I0687049

LEE

BOOK SIX
IN THE LANDON SAGA

A SOLSTICE WESTERN

BY AWARD WINNING AUTHOR
TELL COTTEN

1

Lee

Tell Cotten

Also by Tell Cotten

(The Landon Saga books)
Confessions of a Gunfighter
Entwined Paths
Cooper
Rondo
Yancy

Dedication
To Uncle Lee and Aunt Gaye

Illustrator: Bill Olivas
www.billolivas.com
wbolivas@yahoo.com

Cover design:
Marcy Meinke/Converse Printing & Design
www.ConversePrinting.com
mike@converseprinting.com

Publisher's Note:

This is a work of fiction. All names, characters, places, and events are the work of the author's imagination.

Any resemblance to real persons, places, or events is coincidental.

Solstice Publishing - www.solsticepublishing.com

Author's note

LEE has continued storylines from past books in The Landon Saga series. While it can be read as a stand alone, it is recommended that new readers start with the first book in the series, CONFESSIONS OF A GUNFIGHTER.

Prologue

My name is Lee Mattingly. I'm tall, thin, and ruggedly handsome. Last time I figured it, I was in my mid-thirties.

I'm not as legendary as the Landons, but most folks still know who I am. And, almost everybody's opinion of me is that I need to have my neck lengthened.

I've often been described in newspapers as a rough, mean gunfighter of the west. Sort of a sidekick, you understand, to the *really* bad outlaws. I've ridden with Ben Kinrich, Rondo Landon, and the Oltman brothers, and we've robbed stagecoaches, payrolls, banks, and even rustled a few cows.

I reckon there is some truth to all of that, but I've never considered myself to be quite as bad as they've made me out to be. I've always had a different set of values than most outlaws, and I'm extremely loyal.

I've also always had a conscience, and it's bothered me a lot over the years. The problem is that I've always had a difficult time deciding what's right and what's wrong.

Most folks would be quick to say I'm wrong. However, I've never had to listen to their consciences, just *mine*.

It's also been said that I'm mighty handy with a Colt, and there's no denying the fact that I've killed a lot of men. In fact, I've killed some men that didn't do anything wrong, except for maybe shoot at me. Why they were shooting at me is something we don't need to discuss.

I think that's one of the reasons why I fit in so well during the war. It was permitted and even encouraged to shoot folks that were shooting at me then, but folks feel a lot different about that now that the war's over.

To me it's never been much different, and I've struggled to keep it all straight. And then, soon as it's explained to me, somebody goes and changes all the rules again.

Take the Texas police force. Governor Davis organized them when he took office, and they were supposed to fight crime and help with frontier defense. But, they were corrupt from the start, and Governor Davis used them to arrest anyone that opposed him.

The police force was mostly ex-Yankee soldiers, and they ruled over us old Confederates with no mercy. In fact, the only honest ones in the bunch were Yancy and Cooper Landon over at Midway.

The police force was a natural enemy, and I was just figuring that out when Richard Coke defeated Governor Davis in the election of 1873. The police force was disbanded, and towns went back to electing sheriffs. There was also some talk of the Texas Rangers being reorganized, and that was bad news for men in my line of work.

I was asked once when it was that I went bad. I replied and said that I objected to the notion that I *went* bad. However, if I had to pick, I reckon it was during my youth.

I was born in Kentucky in 1841, and I was raised by Thomas and Sue Mattingly.

Not many folks know this, but there's some mystery concerning my childhood.

I was near ten years old when I overheard Ma say that they weren't my natural parents. I was confused, and Pa vigorously denied it when I asked him about it. Later Pa and Ma had a big argument, and Ma never mentioned it again. Then Ma got sick and died a year later, so I figured I'd never learn the truth.

Jethro, one of Pa's slaves, finally told me. He said he and my Pa were headed home when a big rain came, and they rode up to a draw that was flooding. They had to wait for the water to go down, and that's when I came along. My shirt was snagged on a board, and I was floating down the draw. I got hung up in some bushes, and Jethro swam out and grabbed me. There was nobody else around, so Pa decided to take me home.

I was only two or three years old when it happened, so naturally I don't remember any of it. I asked Jethro if he knew what had happened to my real parents, and he said he didn't.

When I got older I poked around some, but there weren't any answers to be found. And, I still don't know to this day who my real parents are.

I didn't tell Pa that I knew the truth. It would have only caused trouble, and Pa could get ugly sometimes.

My Pa was a mighty stern man. As long as he got what he wanted, he was mostly honest. He was also a crude businessman; he always came out on top.

Pa owned one of the largest tobacco plantations in Kentucky. He was well-known for his tobacco, and he sold his crops back east in all the major cities.

Running a plantation was hard work, and slaves were the cheapest form of labor. Most of the time, Pa treated his slaves decent. However, he was very firm, and he didn't allow any nonsense.

I grew up working amongst the slaves, and they sort of accepted me as one of their own. Pa didn't like it, me hanging around them all the time, but I did it anyway.

Pa loved that plantation, and he decided that I should love it too. By the time I was old enough to hold a hoe, Pa had one ready for me.

A few blisters later, I figured out right quick that I didn't care for being a tobacco farmer. There had to be an easier way to make a living, and I was determined to find it.

One thing I did love early in life was smoking cigars. Pa kept a full box on his desk, and I'd sneak in there when he was out and grab a couple. By the time I was grown, I had probably smoked more cigars than most men ever will.

As I got older, my relationship with Pa took a turn for the worse. He was determined to make me a tobacco farmer, and I was determined *not* to become a tobacco farmer. We argued a lot, and I even ran away from home a time or two.

While I hated farming, I discovered that I had a great love for the game of poker. Jethro taught me how to play, and during my childhood I became an expert poker player.

I was in my teens when I finally discovered an easier way of making a living. I had gone to town for some supplies, and there was a poker game going on in the back of the general store. Curiosity got the best of me, and I sat down and watched.

There was a lot of money in that game, and I figured out real quick that none of them were as good at poker as I was. By the time the deal had gone around a couple of times, I had already picked out all their bad habits.

I reckon I looked eager, because one of them asked if I wanted to play. I said I did, and he asked me if I had any money. I pulled out three dollars from my pocket, and he smiled and said sit down. I did, and two hours later I left with over fifty dollars.

That day changed my life. In just two hours, I made more money than I'd ever had before. It made me feel important, and I liked that feeling.

From then on, I started going to the nearest towns and playing poker in the saloons. Pa didn't like that, so I had to be sneaky about it.

I made a lot of money during those years. I also gained a reputation, and folks traveled from all over to play me. I never lost back then, and I never cheated either.

I was almost twenty years old when a professional gambler came to town. I was late that day, and the game had already started by the time I got there.

The game was crowded, so I sat in the back and watched.

Besides the gambler, there were five other players. Four of these players were plantation owners, and there was more money than usual on the table.

10

The gambler was from Boston, and he spoke with a thick, eastern accent. He wore a town hat, a fancy vest, and had white, slick hands.

This was the first professional gambler I had ever seen, and I enjoyed watching him.

He knew what he was doing. At first he lost more than he was winning, but then he gradually got to winning. About an hour later, he was winning every hand.

A couple of the players had the sense to get out before they lost it all, but three of the plantation owners didn't. By the time the gambler was through with them, they were lucky to have a horse to ride home on.

I reckon I was the only one who could tell that this gambler was stacking the deck and dealing off the bottom. I could have said something, but I didn't. The way I saw it is that they were all grown men, and they could have stopped playing if'n they had wanted to.

It was late by the time the game was over, and there were a lot of sad faces. The gambler smiled and started counting his money as everybody left.

I stayed in the back until the room had cleared out, and it was then that the gambler noticed me.

"Who are you?" He asked.

"Lee Mattingly."

"I've heard of you," he said thoughtfully. "You're a bit younger than I expected."

"You sure know how to handle a deck of cards," I said.

"I'm not sure how to take that," he smiled, and asked, "Do you want to play a few hands, just you and me?"

I didn't reply as I stood.

Now, I don't know when it happened, but something snapped inside of me earlier, and I already knew what I was going to do.

Without a word I drew my pistol, and the gambler's eyes grew wide.

"What's this?" He demanded.

11

"What does it look like?"

"You're robbing me?"

"No, you already did that," I said. "You've been cheating all night."

"Say's who?"

"I know a cardsharp when I see one," I replied, and I cocked the hammer. "You wanna call me a liar?"

"Now hold on," he said desperately. "We can work something out."

"We can," I agreed. "You walk out of here without that cash, and I won't shoot you. I'll also wait until tomorrow to let everyone know they were cheated. That should give you enough time to leave and never come back."

The gambler was caught, and we both knew it. Without a word he stood and walked out, and he left all that money on the table.

At first my intention was to give the money back. But, as I thought on that, I could see the trouble it would cause. Folks would start arguing over how much money they had, and so forth. I'd also have to explain how I got the money.

I didn't want to lie, so I decided to just keep all that money for myself. I figured that was best for everyone involved.

Everything would have worked out fine if it hadn't been for the bartender. Seems like he saw the whole thing, and he took out for the sheriff soon as I rode out of town.

The sheriff had a young deputy by the name of Yancy Landon. Yep, *that* Yancy. They took out after the gambler, and there was a big gunfight when they caught him. The gambler killed the sheriff, but Yancy killed the gambler.

Yancy was promoted to sheriff right after that, and his brother Cooper became his deputy.

The plantation owners felt like I had cheated them somehow, and they wanted their money back. Yancy's first assignment as sheriff was to get it.

Looking back now, I don't blame Yancy for coming after me. After all, it was his job. And, just like everything else in life, Yancy took his job seriously.

I won't go into all the details, but the short version is that I lost the money but still managed to escape.

From that day on I was known as an outlaw, and Yancy has had a strong dislike for me ever since.

I still proclaim my innocence regarding the gambler. After all, I'm not the one who robbed all of those folks. How I see it is that an opportunity presented itself, and I took advantage of it.

If I had it to do all over again, I would have still done the same thing. My only regret is that I didn't kill that bartender. I've never liked folks that stick their nose in other folk's business.

I was now a wanted man, and I had to leave home. Pa was mighty ashamed of me, and he told me to never come back. He also said that I wasn't his real son anyways. I told him I already knew that, and I also told him that I hated being a tobacco farmer. He called me ungrateful, and we left it at that. I rode out and never went back.

I drifted south, and the Civil War broke out a few months later. At the time I was in trouble with the law again, and I was sort of forced into joining up.

For the next four years, I was a loyal soldier for the South. And, even though there were some rough times, I enjoyed my time during the war. I reckon it was the first time in my life that I actually fought for something I believed in.

I met some fine folks in the army, including J.T. Tussle and Noley Landon. Noley was from Louisiana, and he was Rondo's Pa. Rondo was only ten or so at the time, and he was back home on their small farm in Louisiana.

The first couple of years were real rough on our outfit. It seemed like we lost one captain after another, and each new captain kept getting younger and more reckless.

13

Our last captain was brave but not too smart. He led us into an ambush that a blind horse could have seen, and he was the first one killed.

Yancy and Cooper were fighting for the North, and Yancy was a captain. It was his bunch that jumped us, and they hit us hard. Our outfit was wiped out, and the only survivors were Tussle, Noley, and me.

Noley and Tussle were wounded and couldn't travel. We holed up, and I did my best to cover our tracks. But I couldn't fool Cooper, and we were captured the next day.

If it hadn't been for Noley, we would have been sent up north to prison to sit out the war.

Noley was Yancy's uncle, and it was a strained family reunion. After some visiting, Noley made it known that Rondo was all alone down in Louisiana, and that he was sure worried about him.

That wasn't exactly true. Young Uncle Elliot was staying with Rondo, but Noley didn't mention that.

Noley finally got around to asking Yancy if he would let us go. He promised to hightail it to Louisiana and not fight anymore.

At first Yancy said no, but he changed his mind later on. I'm not sure, but I'd bet that Cooper had something to do with that.

If Noley and Tussle hadn't been injured, I would have still been on the first train north. But they needed help, and I made sure that Yancy knew I was available and willing.

Looking back now, I can see how hard of a decision it was for Yancy. He broke the rules, and Yancy never breaks the rules.

Long as I've known him, Yancy has always followed a strict code of ethics. According to him, there's only black or white with no gray in the middle.

I've always found Yancy to be amusing. He takes life so seriously, and he rarely smiles. I've always been a thorn in

14

his side, and I take great pleasure in taking full advantage of that.

Noley hurried home, but Tussle and I joined up with another outfit. And, as luck would have it, we bumped into Yancy again. He took it personal, us being back in the war, and I had to remind him that it was Noley that promised to go home, not us.

But that's not how Yancy remembered it, and he's held a grudge against me ever since.

After the war, I drifted west and ended up in Texas. Along the way I played a lot of poker in the saloons, and I got into a couple of gunfights. Mostly, they were over cardsharps.

By then I was known as a gunfighter. I didn't really consider myself to be one, but that's how it was.

It was during this time that I met Brian Clark, and we've worked together several times during the past few years.

Brian is in his mid-fifties. He's a grizzled veteran outlaw, and he's wanted in nearly every territory or state there is.

Brian and I are alike in a lot of ways. He's loyal, and he has a gentle-like way about him. He's always careful; he never takes any chances unless he has to.

It was Brian that persuaded me to join up with Ben Kinrich, and that's when I met Rondo. By now he was around fifteen, and Brian and I sort of looked after him.

Not that he needed looking after. He was and still is mighty handy with that fancy Colt of his, and his speed is right up there with the best.

Over the years, an unspoken friendship has evolved between Rondo and me. We both struggle with the same things, and we understand each other.

I like to think about things, and I've often wondered who's best with a Colt between Rondo, Yancy, and me. Rondo just laughs when I bring it up, but to me it's an interesting question.

Rondo and I became household names during our years with Ben Kinrich. And, I reckon the newspapers were right. We robbed stagecoaches, payrolls, banks, and rustled cows. But then Kinrich went crazy, and Rondo killed him.

Soon after that, Rondo quit the outlaw life. He went to work as a ranch hand for Mr. Tomlin, and that's where he met Mr. Tomlin's daughter, Rachel.

Rondo tried to talk me into quitting the outlaw life, but I wasn't ready to give it up. I got involved with the Oltman brothers, and I still regret that decision. The Oltman brothers were no good, and they almost got me killed.

It was during this time that I met Jessica Tussle. She was J.T. Tussle's niece, and Cliff Curtis had just kidnapped her. She also had a carpetbag with thousands of dollars in it.

Jessica was in her early twenties. She had a good figure, long blond hair, and light blue eyes. And, as I soon found out, she also had a feisty and persuasive personality.

I'll admit that I've always been fond of Jessica. But, I've never allowed myself to think that anything could ever happen. She's a lady, and I'm an outlaw and a killer. And, I also have suspicions that she's interested in Yancy.

I knew Cliff Curtis from my days with Kinrich. And, even though I disapproved of the situation, I didn't figure it was any of my business.

But that all changed when Jessica offered to pay me a huge sum of money to rescue her. I reckon she was desperate, because she also hired Brian Clark.

I won't go into all the details, but the short version is that we rescued Jessica but lost the money.

Jessica wanted her money back, and she offered Brian and me a share of it if we could find it. Course, I had thoughts of keeping it all for myself, but I just couldn't do it. Brian couldn't do it either, and when we found the carpetbag we rode all the way to Midway and gave it to Jessica.

16

It was the first honest thing either one of us had done in quite a while. It was a good feeling, and it was while we were feeling honorable that Jessica sprang a trap on us that would change our lives.

We met Jessica in her hotel room. I handed her the carpetbag, and my heart melted a bit when she smiled at us.

"There's a lot of money here," she said as she held the carpetbag.

"Sure is," we agreed.

"What do you plan on doing with your share?"

We were silent as we tried to think up a good lie, but I finally smiled sheepishly and shrugged.

"We'll probably whoop it up a little," I admitted. "Do you want me to explain it more than that?"

"No, that explains it well enough," Jessica frowned disapprovingly.

Brian and I were ashamed, and we suddenly became very interested in the floor.

Jessica waited a moment, and then she unleashed her plan.

"My father was a shrewd business man," she said. "And, so am I."

"I would agree with that," I said.

"He taught me a lot about business affairs," Jessica continued. "But, I am a woman in a man's world. I need help."

"What do you have in mind?" I asked.

"I want the three of us to invest this money into a hotel," Jessica declared. "And I mean a very fancy hotel, with a restaurant and a poker room. A hotel that will make us all a lot of money."

"A hotel?" I asked, surprised.

"I want to build the fanciest hotel Texas has ever seen," Jessica continued. "I want it to be an elegant and respectable business. Nothing shady or dishonest."

"No saloon girls?" I smiled.

17

"That is correct," Jessica declared.

"What would you want us to do?" Brian spoke up.

"I want you two to operate the hotel," Jessica explained. "I would be the majority owner with sixty percent. You two would receive twenty percent each, and you'd also receive a monthly salary."

"I don't know a thing about the hotel business," I objected.

"I've heard you are a very good poker player," Jessica said.

"You heard right," I smiled.

"You would run the poker room, and Brian would operate the hotel and restaurant."

Jessica glanced at Brian.

"Didn't you once run your own hotel in El Paso?"

"I did," he nodded, and added, "But it wasn't elegant."

"I'm sure you could do it," Jessica replied.

"What would you do?" I wanted to know.

"I would remain a silent partner," Jessica announced. "I don't want anyone, including my Uncle, to know I am involved."

Brian glanced at me, and it was silent as we thought on that.

"So, what do you think?" Jessica asked. "This is your chance to quit the outlaw business and make an honest living."

"Playing poker everyday doesn't sound too bad," I said. "I'm in if Brian's in."

Jessica looked at him.

"Brian?"

"I ain't getting any younger," he admitted. "And, the outlaw business just ain't what it used to be. It'd be nice to sleep under a roof every night. So, I'm in."

Jessica smiled, and she walked forward and shook our hands.

"Partners it is then," she said.

"Yes, ma'am," I smiled.

"One last thing," she said. "I don't want this hotel to be here in Midway. I have-," she paused and smiled, "-other interests here, and I don't want this hotel to get in the way of that."

"What other interests?" I asked.

"That's for me to know," she replied.

"I think I could guess," I said, and I forced a smile as Yancy came to mind.

"So, that means we need to choose another location," Jessica said as she ignored my comment.

It was silent as we thought on that, and then I snapped my fingers.

"I know the perfect town," I announced.

"Where?" Jessica asked anxiously.

"It's a cow town that should bring in plenty of money on paydays," I explained. "Place called Empty-lake."

"That's where Rondo is from," Jessica recalled.

"Yes," my eyes twinkled, "it sure is."

***

So that's pretty much my life story, give or take a few killings I might have forgot to mention.

After our talk with Jessica, Brian Clark and I took her money and headed south. We bought land in Empty-lake and hired a construction crew, and it took us three months to build the hotel.

It was now two days before our grand opening. And, just as Jessica had wanted, our hotel was the fanciest in Texas.

We had a wedding to go to tomorrow, and then I planned on spending the rest of the day polishing up on my poker skills. I hadn't had much time to play poker these past few months, and I was determined to make a profit on the first night.

19

As I've looked back on my life, I can clearly see the different forks in the road that I've come across. And, I'll admit that most of the time, I've gone in the wrong direction.

However, I felt like I was finally on the right trail. And this time, I was going to do everything honest. Or, at least as honest as possible.

Chapter one

"I now pronounce you husband and wife in the presence of God and these assembled witnesses," the preacher said.

Loud applause passed through the crowd, and Rondo Landon's face turned slightly red. But then Rachel's eyes twinkled at him, and Rondo's confidence returned.

I sat in the back of the church beside Brian Clark. My arms were crossed, and I was deep in thought. This was Rondo's day, but I still couldn't help but imagine myself up there.

It was a startling thought. And, I suddenly realized that it was also an intriguing thought.

Brian glanced at me and noticed my frown.

"What's the matter?" He whispered.

"Nothing," I said quickly.

"Can you believe this?" Brian chuckled. "Who would have thought this possible a few years ago?"

I nodded.

"Rondo's come a long way."

"Poor fellow doesn't know what he just signed up for."

I managed to smile and nod, but my thoughts drifted to Jessica. I wondered where she was, and what she was doing. I also wondered if she ever thought of me.

I had never thought of marriage much, mainly because a man in my line of work couldn't settle down. However, considering the recent changes in my life, marriage was now a possibility I could consider.

Noise interrupted my thoughts, and I noticed that everyone was standing. Rondo and Rachel stood in the front, and a line was forming to congratulate them.

Brian and I stayed in the back. The line finally thinned, and Rondo walked over to us.

Like Yancy, Rondo was smaller than most and had a hard, lean body. And, even though it was his wedding day, he still displayed his ivory handled Colt on his hip, and he also wore his sheriff's badge.

"Congratulations, Button," I smiled.

"I haven't been called that in a while," Rondo smiled back.

"I reckon that nickname doesn't fit much anymore," I figured.

"I reckon not."

"Still, I like to use it every now and then," I said, and my eyes twinkled.

"I've noticed that."

I gestured at Rachel, who was across the room.

"Does she ever call you that?"

"No," Rondo smiled sheepishly. "She doesn't even know about it."

"I could talk to her," I offered.

"Let's not," Rondo said, and we both chuckled.

It was silent for a moment, and then I cleared my throat.

"You've married a beautiful woman, Rondo."

"I know."

"After all you've been through these past years, you deserve this," I said, and Brian nodded.

"I appreciate you saying that."

"You've lived quite a life," I recalled.

Rondo shook his head as he watched Rachel walking towards us.

"No, my life's just beginning," he declared.

Chapter two

I didn't stay at the church long. Soon as I could, I grabbed my hat and slipped out.

I smiled as I walked down the street towards our hotel. It was the tallest building in town, and it could be seen from all directions.

There was a porch that lined the front. The paint was fresh and had a shiny look, and there were more windows than I could count. There was also a huge sign that read 'The Palace Hotel'.

I stepped up onto the porch and unlocked the doors. It was a corner entrance, and there were heavy oak doors on the outside. The oak doors could be opened back in good weather, and there was another set of swinging doors just past them.

I walked through the batwing doors, stopped, and took in the view.

The hotel had two stories. The hotel rooms were upstairs, and there was a balcony that circled three sides of the hotel. All of the rooms upstairs opened up from the balcony.

The restaurant and poker room were downstairs.

Along the length of one wall was an elaborate mahogany bar with a huge, fancy mirror behind it. Bottles and glasses were stacked behind the bar in decorative pyramids.

I was very proud of that mirror. It had come all the way from Dallas, and it was rumored to be the biggest mirror in Texas. It was heavy too. I knew from experience, because I helped carry the thing in.

Along the other wall were a few gaming tables, and behind that was the poker room. In the middle of the room were some tables and chairs, and there was also a fancy chandelier hanging from the ceiling that, when lit, would light up the entire room.

Against the back wall was a fancy spiral staircase that split in two directions. There was a door underneath the stairs that led to the office.

The floors were polished, the mirror gleamed, the glassware sparkled, and the bar shined. It made me proud, and it also gave me a strong feeling of accomplishment.

I grabbed a couple of cigars from the bar, and then I walked to the poker room and sat at a table. I lit my cigar, grabbed a deck of cards, and shuffled. I handled them a bit, and then I dealt myself a hand.

A half an hour later, I was still handling those cards when I heard a noise. I looked up and spotted Rondo standing inside the doorway.

"What are you doing here?" I asked.

"You left, and I wanted to say goodbye," Rondo explained.

"You going somewhere?"

"We're headed to San Antonio. We'll be back in a few weeks."

"Taking a honeymoon?"

"Something like that."

"Want me to come along?"

"I do not," Rondo smiled, and we both chuckled.

"You'll miss our grand opening tomorrow night," I tried to look hurt.

"I'm sure things will be fine."

"What if we have trouble?"

"Ross will be here. I'm sure you, Brian, and Ross can handle anything that comes up."

"I reckon we can," I smiled.

Rondo nodded as he looked around.

"First time I've seen the inside," he commented.

"What do you think?"

"You've done yourself proud, Lee."

"I'm satisfied with the results," I agreed.

"You should be," Rondo said, and asked, "Why'd you put the entrance in the corner?"

"It's hard to leave when you can't find the door," I explained.

Rondo smiled and shook his head.

"I reckon you have a point," he chuckled, and added, "I understand now why you named it The Palace Hotel. It sure is mighty fancy."

"It's what Jessica wanted."

"Jessica? She's your silent partner?" Rondo looked surprised.

I scowled, and muttered, "You weren't supposed to know that."

"I won't say anything," Rondo reassured, and asked, "Does Yancy know?"

"Not that I know of."

"Be interesting if he found out."

"Could be," I agreed.

Rondo smiled. It was silent for a moment, and then he turned towards the door.

"Well, Rachel's waiting."

"Have a good trip, Rondo."

"I plan to."

He paused at the door and looked back at me. I smiled, and then he was gone.

Chapter three

Brian Clark and I shared a room upstairs in the hotel. It was a corner room, and we had a good view of the town from our window.

We were up early the next morning, and after breakfast I went outside while Brian had a meeting with our hotel employees.

I was glad Brian was handling that part of the hotel. For some reason all the employees were timid around me, and they seemed more comfortable around Brian.

I strolled down the street and spotted Ross Stewart sitting on the porch at the sheriff's office. He was drinking coffee while he studied a chessboard.

Ross had a tall and lanky frame, with tanned skin and brown hair. When he spoke he always displayed a rich, Texan drawl.

Ross was Rondo's deputy.

They had met when Rondo went to work for Mr. Tomlin. At the time, they were both fond of Rachel. But Rachel chose Rondo, and that was that. A lot of friendships might have ended, but they were able to overcome it, and they were still close friends.

In some ways, Ross reminded me of Yancy. He was extremely honest, and he was always curious about this or that.

We got along all right, but I had suspicions that deep down, Ross was wary of me.

"Morning, Ross," I said as I walked up.

Ross looked up from his chessboard and spotted me.

"Lee," he nodded.

"Who's winning?" I smiled and gestured at the game.

"I'm just studying up for when Rondo gets back," Ross explained. "I taught him the game a while back, and now I can't seem to beat him anymore."

26

"The pupil has gotten better than the teacher?"

"Something like that."

"Rondo does that sometimes," I said, and I smiled as Ben Kinrich came to mind.

Ross grunted and gestured at the coffee pot.

"Coffee?"

"Thanks," I nodded.

I grabbed a cup, poured myself some coffee, and sat next to Ross.

"Do you play?" Ross motioned at the chessboard.

"No, I'm a poker player."

"So is Rondo," Ross said, and added sourly, "Now, he beats me at both."

I chuckled, and it was silent while we drank our coffee.

"Are you ready for the grand opening?" Ross asked after a while.

"I think so."

"Think there'll be trouble?"

"I doubt it."

"What if Ike's men show up?"

That was a sobering thought, and I frowned thoughtfully.

"I hadn't thought of that," I admitted.

"I'll be ready if you need me," Ross declared.

Ross wasn't near as good with a Colt as Rondo or me, but I appreciated the gesture.

"Thanks," I said, and Ross nodded.

After that it was silent, and my thoughts drifted to Ike Nash.

Ike was a businessman. All he cared about was how to make a profit, and he was very shrewd and cunning. He had been deeply involved with Governor Davis's schemes, but he had the good sense to get out before it caved on him.

Since then, he'd been running things on his own. All across Texas he had created his own little empire, and he was involved in several businesses.

Everything he did was illegal, including trading rifles to the Indians. However, Ike had it set up so that nothing could be traced back to him.

Ike was the reason Rondo was sheriff. He owned a nearby ranch, and his men kept coming to town and stirring up trouble on paydays. At the time there was no law, so the town council hired Rondo.

Not long after that, Ike's son Tanner killed Jeremiah Batch. Rondo arrested him and sent for Judge Parker. But, before Judge Parker arrived, Tanner escaped with the help of Virgil Carson and Lucy Wells. Rondo hired me as a special deputy, and we took out after them.

It didn't take us long to catch them. Virgil and Tanner were killed, and Lucy was now a guest at Huntsville prison. She swore she'd get revenge, but we were more worried about how Ike would react. However, we hadn't seen much of Ike or his men, so all was well for now.

Personally, I thought Ike was scared of us. However, I'd been wrong before, and I knew that we'd better be ready, just in case.

I finished my coffee with a gulp. I stood, set my cup down, and looked at Ross.

"Thanks for the coffee."

"Anytime," Ross said.

I nodded and headed for the hotel.

Chapter four

Ike Nash ate breakfast as he usually did, sitting behind his desk in his study.

It was an impressive room, and it was also where Ike spent most of his time. There was a fireplace, and there was also the smell of cigar smoke in the air.

Ike's ranch was roughly five miles south of town, and Ike was proud of the place.

The headquarters was in a meadow, beside a stream. The pole pens, bunkhouse, and main house were all new and well built.

Ike was a big, solid man. Deep voiced, wide shouldered, and tall, he had a commanding presence that made most folks uncomfortable.

He was also very good with a Colt. However, he kept this to himself, and even Butch, his right hand man, didn't know how good he really was.

Ike took a swig of coffee and leaned back in his chair. There was a noise by the door, and Butch Nelson appeared.

Butch was a plain-looking man. Short with a broad face, he looked more like a storekeeper.

But he was far from that. He was very good with a Colt, and he displayed one on his hip. However, even with the Colt, there was still nothing that really stood out. And, that's exactly how Butch preferred it.

"Morning, Ike."

"Butch."

"There's news from town. I thought you'd be interested."

"What is it?" Ike raised an eyebrow.

"Rondo Landon got married. He's gone to San Antonio on a honeymoon."

Ike grunted in displeasure.

"Well, I hope he enjoys himself."

"Do you still hold a grudge against him regarding Tanner?"

"I do," Ike nodded, and asked, "Is there anything else?"

"Yes. Lee Mattingly's hotel is opening tonight."

"Well now. That's interesting," Ike looked intrigued. "Where's that gambler we sent for?"

"He should be here any day now."

"How about the other man. What's his name?"

"Amos," Butch said, and added, "He's right where we want him."

"Are you sure he's good enough?"

"He came highly recommended. He's good at what he does."

"He'd better be," Ike declared. It was silent, and he added, "Interesting, Lee's hotel opening tonight, and Rondo isn't here."

"I found that interesting too."

"Perhaps some of the men should pay the hotel a visit tonight," Ike suggested. "I want to see how prepared Lee is."

"Want me to go along?"

"No, I don't want you involved. Tell Brock to go. He'll like that."

"I'll tell him," Butch said, and he walked towards the door.

"Butch," Ike called out.

"Yes?" Butch paused at the doorway.

"Tell Brock not to get too rough. After all, I'm going to own that hotel before long."

"Yes, sir," Butch said, and then he was gone.

Ike grunted in satisfaction. He took a swig of coffee and returned to his breakfast.

30

Chapter five

I walked back to the hotel.

Brian was still meeting with the hotel employees. I motioned at him, and he nodded. I stayed in the back until he had finished.

"Is there anything else you need to add?" Brian looked at me.

"As a matter of fact, there is," I said, and I walked up front and stood beside Brian.

The room was quiet, and everyone watched me. I had never talked much, and everybody looked curious. I smiled at them and cleared my throat.

"Can anybody here shoot?"

They glanced uncertainly at each other and looked back at me.

"We ain't gunfighters," one of them said.

"I can tell that," I smiled patiently. "But can anybody shoot?"

"Shoot what?" The same person asked.

"Possible troublemakers."

"You expecting trouble?"

"No, but I want to be prepared for it."

The speaker was tall, muscular, and red headed. Nobody else said anything, so he took charge.

"I think I speak for everyone when I say I didn't hire on to shoot folks," he said, and everybody else nodded. "We ain't like you," he added.

"And what am I?" I frowned.

"You know. A gunfighter."

"Is that all you think I am?"

"You've helped several undertakers pay their bills," he declared.

It was silent as I thought on that, and I nodded slowly.

"Yes, I reckon I have," I admitted.

"If you're worried about trouble, perhaps you should have hired a few gunmen like yourself," the red headed man suggested, and added, "It's unfair to ask us common folks to defend your hotel. We aren't killers like you."

"What's your name?" I narrowed my eyes.

"Amos. Amos Gregg."

"I get the feeling, Amos, that you don't like me."

"I don't dislike you. I just know what you are."

"What I am-," I paused for effect, "-is your boss. I'd like you to remember that."

"Oh, I'll remember."

It fell silent as Amos and I stared at each other. A few awkward seconds passed, and I looked around at everybody else. They all dropped their eyes when I made eye contact.

"This was a good talk," I said wryly, and then I glanced at Brian. "I'll be in the office if you need me."

Nobody said a word as I left.

Chapter six

I sat behind my desk and grabbed a cigar. I trimmed it carefully, and Brian Clark entered the room as I lit it and took a deep puff.

"What was that all about?" Brian asked me.

I didn't reply. I took in a big breath and let it out slowly, and my faced was pinched in thought.

"You there?" Brian looked at me strangely.

"Sorry," I said as I recovered. "I was deep in thought."

"I didn't know you were such a thinker."

"Only as a last resort."

"What were you thinking about?"

"Amos," I said. "He sure speaks his mind."

"So do you," Brian pointed out.

"True, but I usually make sense."

"All of our employees are worried now."

"Worried about what?"

"Worried they're going to get shot at," Brian explained. "Amos is still talking out there."

"I don't like Amos," I announced. "Mebbe we should fire him."

"For what?" Brian looked surprised.

"I just told you I don't like him."

"We can't fire him because of that," Brian objected.

"Why not?"

"The rest of the men look up to him. Amos goes, and they might all leave."

I sighed as I thought on that.

"This boss thing is more complicated than I thought," I complained.

"You just focus on poker and leave the men to me," Brian instructed. "And, from here on out, just come to me with any concerns you have. I'll handle it."

I scowled.

"So, in other words, you want me to be more like Yancy and keep quiet."

"Exactly."

"Why's everybody so scared of me?" I wanted to know.

"Your reputation might have something to do with it," Brian suggested.

I grunted and shook my head.

"A bunch of school boys would be tougher than that bunch out there. First mention of trouble and they're already looking for a place to hide."

"Labor is scarce in these parts," Brian reminded. "I had to take what I could find."

I grunted again, and it fell silent.

"Why the sudden worry?" Brian asked.

"Ross mentioned Ike Nash."

A thoughtful look crossed Brian's face.

"You think he'd cause trouble?"

"I doubt it, but it is a possibility."

"Then don't you think we'd better get prepared?" Brian looked concerned.

"That's what I was *trying* to do," I frowned, and then I scratched my jaw in thought. "If there is any trouble, it's probably just going to be you, me, and Ross."

"Probably so."

"Well then. I reckon we're about as prepared as we can get."

"There'd better not be too much trouble. We can't afford it," Brian warned.

"What do you mean?" I narrowed my eyes.

Brian gestured at the safe that was behind me in the corner.

"Have you looked in there lately?"

"No," I admitted.

"We've been squeezing dimes to get dollars these past few weeks, and now we barely have any pennies left,"

Brian informed. "We have just enough for payroll. All the money from Jessica is gone."

"What happened to the dimes?"

"You'll be playing poker with them," Brian retorted, and added, "We'll be all right once we get some money coming in, but be careful tonight. You lose big, and we won't be able to cover it."

"What if I'm rusty?" I objected.

"Don't be."

I frowned as Brian walked towards the door.

"I'd better make sure nobody quit," he said. "See you later."

"I'm sorry if I caused any trouble," I called out after him. "I reckon I'm just getting irritable."

"Getting?" Brian smiled, and I scowled as he walked out.

Chapter seven

The biggest challenge in running a restaurant was finding fresh beef. We made a deal with Mr. Tomlin for a steady supply, and we hired our own butcher and built a butcher block out back. We also built a corral where we could keep our steers.

Brian Clark rode out that afternoon to pick up more steers, and I stayed in the office and practiced handling and shuffling a deck of cards.

It was midafternoon when the door knocked, and in stepped Amos Gregg.

"Boss," he said. "There's a lady and a kid out here wanting to see you."

"Oh?" I asked curiously. "Who is it?"

"She didn't say. They just arrived on the stage."

"All right. Show her in," I said.

Amos nodded and turned to go, but then he stopped.

"I'm sorry about earlier," he said. "I have a bad habit of speaking my mind."

"I noticed that."

"Well, like I said, I'm sorry."

"No you're not," I smiled, and added, "You can bring the lady in now."

Amos frowned, but he didn't say anything as he turned and walked out.

There was only one lady I thought it would be, and I was excited to see her. My only confusion was why she was here, and who the kid was.

I disposed of my cigar, hastily cleaned off my desk, and sat up straight in my chair and tried to look important.

Seconds later the door opened, and in walked a lady and a small child.

To my surprise, the lady was not Jessica. She was a tall, graceful looking woman with tired eyes and a wisp of natural gray hair here and there. It was hard to tell, but I guessed her to be in her early thirties.

As for the child, she was probably around nine or ten. She had long blond hair, and she also had the cutest face I had ever seen.

Her round, blue eyes stared straight into mine. It was a piercing look, and I couldn't help but stare back.

They were both clean and well groomed, but their clothes were worn, and they were very slim. I knew at first glance that they had very little money.

I was startled, and several awkward seconds passed before I cleared my throat.

"You wanted to see me, ma'am?"

The woman spoke with a clear, distinguished voice. She sounded tired but also proud.

"You are Lee Mattingly," she said, and it sounded more like a statement than a question.

"That's me."

"I am April Gibson, and this is my daughter June."

"Where's May?" I made a weak attempt at humor.

"She died last month."

My face turned somber.

"I'm sorry."

"Don't feel bad. You didn't know," she said.

I nodded and looked at June, and she was still staring at me through round and very solemn eyes. I swallowed and looked back at April Gibson.

"Do I know you, ma'am?"

"No, we've never met," she said. "But of course, I know who you are."

I smiled and nodded, and then a thoughtful look crossed my face as I studied her.

"You do look sorta familiar."

"You might have seen me in Midway. That's where we're from."

"And you rode the stage all the way here?"

37

"Yes, we just arrived a while ago."

I nodded, and it was silent for several long seconds.

"So, what can I do for you, ma'am?" I finally asked.

"I need a job. I was hoping you would give me one."

"To do what?" I asked, confused.

"I can wash dishes, mop floors, do laundry, clean the rooms; anything," she said. It was silent, and she added sternly, "Almost anything."

I smiled faintly.

"I don't mean to intrude, but where's your husband?"

"He's dead," she said, and her voice shook a little.

"Oh?" I asked, startled. "What happened to him?"

"My husband was a shotgun rider for the stage line in Midway," she explained. "He was killed last year when Cliff Curtis and his men held up the stage. Yancy Landon told me later that it was Stew Baine that actually shot him."

I nodded thoughtfully as I remember back.

"Your husband was Sam Gibson."

"That's right."

"I wasn't there, but I heard about it," I said. "Stew also killed the driver."

April didn't say anything. Instead her face turned soft and sad with the memory of an old pain.

"But I was there-," I tried to be helpful, "-when Stew Baine was killed."

April didn't say anything. Instead, she just nodded.

"So, what made you leave Midway?" I prodded for more information.

"After Sam was killed, Yancy helped me find odd jobs around town," she said. "It was tough going, but we made it."

"That's sounds like Yancy."

"But then May got sick and died last month-," April paused as tears came to her eyes, "-and we just couldn't stay there anymore. I sold our house, got on the stage, and came here."

38

"And why did you choose this town?"

"Yancy and Cooper were real nice to me, and they helped me a lot," she said. "I knew their cousin Rondo was here, and I had hoped that he would be able to find me some work. But he's not here, and then I heard that you owned this hotel."

I nodded slowly as I thought on that.

"You'd be the only woman employee," I warned.

"I'm fine with that."

I scratched my jaw. It was very silent, and April's face remained emotionless.

June was still staring at me, and I made the mistake of looking at her. Her piercing eyes made me fidgety.

"All right," I said as I looked back at April. "See Brian Clark when he gets back. He'll find you something to do."

A small smile appeared on her face, but it disappeared just as fast.

"Thank you very much, Mr. Mattingly," she said.

"The name's Lee."

"Yes, sir. I mean, Lee."

I nodded and smiled. I waited for them to leave, but they just stood there.

"Is there anything else?" I finally asked.

"We have nowhere to stay," she explained, and added quietly, "We don't have much money."

"I see," I said thoughtfully, and then I sighed. "All right. You can live upstairs. Brian Clark and I share the corner room, and you can have the room next to ours."

"Thank you, sir."

"Lee," I corrected.

"I'm sorry," she said, and blushed slightly. "Thank you again, Lee."

"No problem."

April nodded and turned towards the door while I grabbed my deck of cards.

39

I still felt a pair of eyes on me. I looked up, and June hadn't moved. She was still staring at me through those round and solemn eyes.

"Mister Lee," she said suddenly, and her voice was very soft and clear.

"Yes?" I said, startled.

"Thank you for giving Ma a job," she said, and then she turned abruptly and followed her mother out the door.

I sat there for a long time in stunned silence.

"You're welcome," I finally said to an empty room.

Chapter eight

Brian Clark burst into the office a couple of hours later.

"Amos told me you just hired a woman," he said gruffly.

"That's right," I confirmed.

"I just told you we can barely meet payroll," he objected. "We can't afford anybody else."

"They have no place else to go," I protested. "And, that ain't all. Wait until you meet June. The way she stared at me, it felt like she was looking into my soul."

Brian snorted.

"They can't stay here, Lee."

"Have you met them yet?"

"No. They're upstairs, getting settled in a room that we won't be able to rent out now."

"Go meet them," I suggested. "And then, if you still want them to leave, get rid of them."

"I'll do that," Brian declared, and he turned and stormed out.

I smiled and waited patiently. A few minutes passed, and Brian returned to the office. He looked sullen and somber.

"Well?" I asked.

"I'll find something for her to do," he muttered.

"June stared at you too, eh?"

"She did," Brian admitted.

I didn't reply. Instead, I just smiled.

***

A few hours later, I stood in front of a mirror up in our room, looking at my reflection.

I had just come from the bathhouse, and I was also freshly shaved. I wore a brand new shirt, new pants, and

41

polished boots. Altogether, I had to admit that I looked quite handsome.

I displayed my Colt on my right hip. It was loaded and ready, but I checked it once more just to be sure.

I grinned at myself in the mirror. I holstered my Colt, grabbed my hat, and walked out.

Outside my room in the hallway, I leaned on the railing and looked below.

I couldn't help but smile. We had only been open for an hour, and already business was booming.

Men were lined up at the bar, and all of the tables were full. Waiters hustled about, serving them. Amos and two others were behind the bar, and April was cleaning tables.

The gaming tables were busy too, and I also noticed several men lingering in the poker room, waiting for a game.

"Jessica would be proud," I said to myself softly as I walked down the stairs.

I exchanged a few pleasantries, and then I made my way over to the poker room. I sat at the center table and smiled at everyone.

"Shall we get started?" I asked.

Several men nodded and walked over.

There was a new deck of cards on the table. While everyone sat down, I grabbed the deck and shuffled.

***

After an hour of playing, I was pretty much even. I had won a few hands, but I'd also lost some.

I finally got the hand I was waiting for. I had a sure winner, and I bet high. Nobody folded, and the pot grew big.

Suddenly, I felt a pair of eyes on me. I glanced behind me, and June stood there, looking at me through those big and solemn eyes.

I was startled, and I almost dropped my cards.

"Mister Lee," she said in that soft and clear voice.

"June, you shouldn't be in here," I said sternly.

"Mister Lee, I gotta go," she said as she ignored my comment.

"Go where?" I frowned.

"I gotta *go*," she said again more urgently.

"Oh. That," I said, and I gestured at the back door. "Go ahead. The outhouse is out there."

"But it's dark," she objected.

"Yes, it does that when the sun goes down."

"Ma told me not to go outside when it's dark."

I frowned at her, but June's face remained the same.

"Where's your Ma?"

"She's busy, cleaning tables."

"Fine," I muttered. "I'll take you. Wait until this hand is over."

The game had come to an abrupt halt. Everyone was watching us, and I noticed a few frowns.

"I'm sorry," I smiled at everybody.

"How many cards?" The dealer asked.

"I'll play these," I said.

The dealer nodded and moved to the next player. I started to look at my cards again, but before I could I felt a tug on my shoulder.

"Mister Lee," June said. "I gotta go bad."

"Wait."

"I can't."

The game had halted again, and everyone was frowning at us.

"You can't wait two minutes?"

"No. I gotta go bad, Mister Lee."

I frowned at her, and she stared back through those round and solemn eyes.

"Fine," I grumbled. "Let's go."

As I stood, I reluctantly tossed my cards facedown onto the table.

"I fold," I said, and added, "I'll be right back."

I heard a few mumblings as I took June by the hand and left.

Chapter nine

"How long does it take for one little girl to go to the outhouse?" I asked irritably.

"I'm almost done, Mister Lee," came the soft and clear voice from inside.

Several minutes had passed, and the night air was cool. I rubbed my shoulders and shivered while I waited.

I finally heard a noise. The outhouse door opened, and June stepped out.

"All done?" I asked as I took her by the hand.

"Yes. Thank you, Mister Lee."

"Don't mention it," I said as we hurried back inside.

April was in the poker room, and she looked worried. But then she spotted us, and a relieved look crossed her face.

"There you are," she said sternly. "Where have you been?"

"She had to go to the outhouse," I explained.

April's eyes grew wide.

"Oh! I'm so sorry," she said as she took June's hand.

"Forget it," I said, and then I gestured at the poker table. "Now if you'll excuse me."

"Yes, of course!" April said, and she hurried out of the room, leading June behind her.

I watched them go, and I sighed as I sat back down at the table.

"Now, where were we?" I asked with a smile.

***

Usually, when I finally got a good hand, that was a sign that other good hands were about to follow. But, not on this night. I started losing hand after hand, and I had to fold a lot. It became irritating and frustrating.

45

Another hour passed, and by then lady luck had completely turned her back on me.

"Deal me out," I said as I stood. "I need some coffee."

The men nodded, and I walked to the front room.

Things were busy. All of the tables were occupied, and the room was loud with laughter and chatter.

I walked over to the bar and caught Amos's attention.

"Coffee," I said.

He nodded. He poured me a cup and set it on the bar in front of me.

"How's the poker game?" He asked.

"Why do you care?" I scowled.

"I'm sorry," he said quickly. "I was just making conversation."

I grunted in response. I took a swig of coffee, and I grimaced as I burned my tongue.

"Hot?" Amos asked.

"Just a little."

"I'm sorry if I made it too hot."

I didn't reply. Instead, I shot Amos a dark look, and he moved down the bar and tended to another customer.

A few minutes passed, and Brian Clark walked over.

"How's the game going?"

"It's going," I grumbled.

Brian frowned thoughtfully. He started to say something, but before he could three men came through the swinging doors. They walked with a swagger and looked arrogant.

I recognized all three. They were Ike Nash's men, and Brock Jackson was leading them.

Brock was one of Ike's top hands. He stood over six feet tall, and he had a muscled torso with dark hair.

I had never liked Brock. He had a cocky way about him, and just about anybody could tell that he had a high opinion of himself.

They paused at the door and looked around.

46

Brock smirked when he spotted us, and then his eyes went on down the bar. His eyes lingered on Amos before he glanced around at the rest of the room.

I narrowed my eyes in suspicion. I wasn't sure, but it looked like Brock had nodded slightly at Amos.

I glanced at Amos. His face was emotionless as he came over to us.

"Those are Ike Nash's men," he told us in a hushed voice. "They might cause trouble."

"That's very good, Amos," I said sarcastically. "If you were a horse, I'd feed you a carrot."

A look of anger crossed his face, but I ignored him as I turned towards Brian.

"When you get the chance, slip out and find Ross," I murmured. "Whatever happens, he should be here."

Brian nodded and moved away from the bar. Meanwhile, I took a swig of coffee and tried to look unconcerned as I watched Brock and his men.

Chapter ten

Brian slipped out the back door while Brock and his men made their way to the other end of the bar. Amos served them drinks, and they leaned against the bar and watched the activity in the room. All three had scornful looks as they sipped their whiskey.

April appeared from the back, and she didn't notice them as she walked by. There was a dirty table near them, and she gathered up the dishes and cleaned the table.

A wolfish look crossed Brock's face as he watched her, and I narrowed my eyes.

April had her hands full as she turned and started towards the kitchen. She was walking briskly, but Brock stepped forward and blocked her path.

"Well! I thought I knew all the girls in town," he scoffed. "Where'd you come from, little lady?"

"Excuse me," I heard April say.

Brock grinned savagely, and several tense seconds passed. He continued to stare at her, but April kept her eyes downward.

Brock finally laughed and stepped back to the bar. April seized the opportunity and hurried past them.

I frowned disapprovingly. Old feelings started to stir within me, but I managed to stay calm.

Brock finished his drink and walked over to the gaming tables. Meanwhile, his two companions searched the tables, looking for a place to sit down.

One of them was tall, and the other one was short. They both wore Colts on their hips, and they looked eager to use them.

All of the tables were taken. They stood there a moment, and I saw them gesture at a table in the back and nod at each other.

There was an elderly couple occupying the table. They sat huddled together as they ate their supper.

The short man and tall man walked up to their table. Their movements were slow and deliberate, and just about everyone saw them. Just like that the room got quiet and still.

The elderly couple was still eating, and they were unaware that anything was happening.

The two men hovered over the table and sneered down at them. Their backs were to me, so I left the bar and walked quietly towards them.

"Hey, old man," I heard Shorty say.

The elderly couple looked up and spotted them.

"Yes?" The elderly man asked.

"You're sitting at our table."

The elderly man stiffened, and a stubborn look crossed his face.

"You are mistaken," he said in a firm voice.

A snarl appeared on Shorty's face.

"You calling me a liar?"

"No, but we're not moving," the elderly man declared.

I now stood directly behind them, and my gun hand hovered naturally over my Colt's handle.

I took a quick glance at Brock. He was standing by the gaming tables, and he had an amused look on his face. But his arms were crossed, and it didn't look like he was going to step in.

Shorty was about to say something when I cleared my throat and got their attention. They turned around, and as they did the elderly couple stood and moved out of the line of fire.

"Well now," Shorty sneered. "If it ain't the great Lee Mattingly."

"That's me."

"I've heard you're *some* hand with a Colt," Shorty scoffed.

"You heard right," I said, and added, "I'll have to ask you boys to leave. Now."

"What for?" Shorty asked, startled.

"Harassing the customers."

"But we just got here," Shorty objected.

"When you got here makes no difference to me," I replied.

They didn't like that. They glanced at each other and looked back at me.

"And if we don't?"

I smiled.

"You boys have two choices. You can walk outta here, or you can be dragged out. Doesn't really matter to me."

"We ain't going nowhere."

I nodded. My shoulders were relaxed, and I was ready.

"You have a reputation and all, but that doesn't matter to us," Shorty sneered. "You ain't nothing special."

"Funny, I was just thinking the same thing about you."

That did it. Shorty's eyes went hard, and he grabbed for his Colt.

Shorty was fast. We cleared leather at the same time, and the sound of our Colts blended together.

My aim was true, but Shorty fired too soon. His bullet tore into the boards at my boots, and I heard a sharp whip as the bullet ricocheted.

There was a sound of broken glass behind me as I jumped sideways.

The tall man had fumbled his draw, and he was just bringing his Colt up when I fired into him. The bullet hit him in the chest with a thud, and he went flying backwards into the back wall.

Shorty was still standing, and he had a shocked look on his face. I started to shoot him again, but he dropped his Colt and crumpled forward before I could.

Meanwhile, the tall man was leaning against the back wall with a dazed look. A hole in his chest oozed blood out as he slumped to the floor.

There was a haze of smoke in the room, and I squinted through it. Near as I could tell, both men were dead.

There was a sound at the door. Brian and Ross appeared behind me, and they held their Colts. Brian covered Brock, who was still standing beside the gaming tables.

A heavy silence held the room while the smoky haze lifted. All eyes were on me as I took the spent shells from my Colt and put new ones in.

I walked over to Brock with my Colt in hand, and Brian and Ross were behind me.

Brock had uncrossed his arms, and his hand hovered over his gun handle. I could tell by the expression on his face that he was tempted to go for it.

"Wave at the angels before you do something stupid," I said sternly.

A confused look crossed his face.

"What?" He asked roughly.

I sighed and explained, "Hold your hands up."

"Oh," Brock said, and he slowly raised his hands to shoulder height. "That was nice shooting, Lee," he drawled.

"You're leaving," I said as I ignored his comment. "Now."

"Why me? I ain't causing any trouble."

"My hotel. My rules."

Brock made an odd snorting sound. I wasn't sure, but I think it was an attempt at a laugh.

"All right. I'll leave if that's what you want."

"That's what I want."

"But I ain't leaving because I'm scared."

"Long as you leave, I don't care what mood you're in."

Brock smiled at that.

"We'll see each other again," he said.

"And I hope you try something too," I replied sarcastically. "I'd enjoy the practice."

Brock grunted in response as he walked towards the door.

Soon as he was gone, Brian glanced at me.

"'Wave at the angels'?" He asked softly.

"I just thought it up on the spot, real quick like," I explained.

"I could tell."

Chapter eleven

Ross wanted to know what happened, so I told him briefly how the events played out. He didn't say much, but I could tell that he disapproved. Afterwards he left, saying that he wanted to write a report so he could fill in Rondo when he returned.

I spotted Amos behind the bar. He had a disturbed look, but he changed expressions when he saw me watching him.

"Amos," I called out. "Go get the undertaker."

"Who? Me?"

"Is there anybody else named Amos working here?" I glared at him.

"Oh. No. I'm sorry," Amos stammered, and he hurried towards the door.

I narrowed my eyes as I watched him.

"Have you noticed how Amos is always apologizing?" I asked Brian in a quiet voice.

"He probably doesn't want to get fired."

"I don't think so," I disagreed. "A man who apologizes all the time means he knows something we don't."

Brian snorted.

"Aw, you're just getting superstitious."

"Time will tell," I replied. It was silent, and I added, "I could use some coffee."

Brian nodded in agreement. I started towards the bar, but then I stopped abruptly. The mirror behind the bar had been shattered, and broken glass was everywhere.

"What happened to our mirror?" My mouth fell open.

"Looks like it got hit," Brian observed.

"I can see *that*," I frowned. "But who did it?"

Brian gestured at the two dead men.

"It was probably one of them."

I shook my head in disgust.

"Of all the things in here, did they have to hit the mirror?" I complained.

"I reckon they could have hit you instead," Brian tried to be helpful.

"That mirror cost a small fortune," I said as I ignored his comment.

"Yes, Lee. I know. I'm the one who paid for it."

I shook my head again and grunted in displeasure.

***

Brian and I sat at our corner table. We were drinking coffee, and I was also smoking a cigar. Our faces were glum as we looked at the wall where our mirror had been.

The excitement had caused all of our customers to leave. The place was a mess, so we closed early.

The undertaker had just arrived. He had two helpers with him, and they rolled Shorty and the tall man up into tarps and dragged them out.

Meanwhile, Amos brought out a mop and started cleaning up the blood while April swept up the broken glass.

I took a swig of coffee as I watched them, and then I sighed.

"Things didn't go so well tonight," I muttered.

"I'll agree with that."

"Things are bound to get better. It can't get any worse."

"It can't?" Brian shot me a questioning look.

"For our sakes, it'd better not," I replied, and asked, "Can we afford to replace the mirror?"

"No," Brian said matter-of-factly. "Least not for a while."

I frowned as I took a deep puff on my cigar.

"The bar looks sorta odd without a mirror."

"We'll get used to it."

54

"When you think about it, having a mirror behind the bar really makes no sense," I reasoned.

"How's that?" Brian glanced at me with a confused look.

"Who wants to stand at the bar and watch himself get drunk?"

Brian pinched his face in thought.

"I can see your point."

I nodded emphatically, and it fell silent as we drank our coffee.

Chapter twelve

Brock Jackson stood in front of Ike's desk. He held his hat with both hands, and his face was solemn as he told Ike what had happened.

Ike sat behind his desk, and Butch stood in the corner. Their faces were emotionless as they listened. Afterwards, the room was very quiet.

Ike cleared his throat. He glanced at Butch and looked back at Brock.

"Did I not make myself clear when I said not to get too rough?"

"You did."

"Then what happened?"

"It wasn't me that started the trouble. It was the other two."

"And now they're dead."

"Yes, sir. They sure are."

It fell silent again as Ike pondered that. After a moment a wolfish smile crossed Ike's face, and Brock relaxed a bit.

"Well, I wanted to know how prepared Lee was, and now I know," Ike said, and then he chuckled.

"I'm sorry, Ike."

"Don't worry about it," Ike waved his hand at him. "It wasn't your fault. Go ahead and turn in."

Brock nodded. He started to leave, but Ike stopped him.

"How fast was Lee?"

"He was real fast," Brock grudgingly admitted.

"Fast as you?"

"I don't think so. But he's smart. Real smart."

Ike grunted, and Brock left the room. Meanwhile, Butch left the corner and walked up to Ike's desk.

"Gather a few men in the morning," Ike told Butch. "I think it's time I paid Lee a visit."

"How many men?"

"Just a few. I don't want Lee thinking I'm afraid of him."

"How about Brock?"

"Not him. I don't want him anywhere near Lee until this is all over. I need him."

"I'll take care of it."

Ike nodded, and Butch left the study.

Chapter thirteen

I couldn't sleep much that night. Instead, I lay in bed and listened to Brian snore.

I finally gave up about an hour before sunrise. I splashed some water in my face, got dressed, and walked out the door.

The hallway was very dark, and I had to be careful as I went down the stairs.

I was surprised to find a light in the kitchen. My hand gripped my Colt, but then I relaxed when I spotted April.

I started to say something, but for some reason I remained quiet. I stayed in the dark and watched her.

She had a fire going in the stove, and she was boiling water in a coffee pot.

I finally cleared my throat. She spun around, and a small smile crossed her lips when she spotted me.

"I'm sorry. Did I scare you?" I asked as I stepped into the light.

"No, I was just making some coffee."

"I can see that," I smiled quizzically. "Who's it for?"

"You."

"Me?" I frowned, surprised.

"I noticed yesterday that you like coffee."

"I'm not addicted to it like the Landons are, but I enjoy a cup every once in while," I agreed.

"I thought I'd have some ready for you when you got up," April explained.

I was surprised, and I scratched my jaw as I studied her.

"Well," I finally said. "You *are* mighty handy to have around."

April looked pleased.

"Go have a seat," she urged. "I'll bring it to you when it's ready."

"Yes, ma'am."

58

I walked back to the main room. A faint light was beginning to show outside as I sat at our corner table.

A few minutes passed, and April appeared from the kitchen with the pot of coffee. She poured me a cup, and she watched anxiously as I took a swig.

"Good coffee," I declared.

"I'm glad you like it," she said, and asked, "Do you get up this time every morning?"

"Depends."

"On what?"

"How loud Brian is snoring," I smiled.

April smiled back.

"I'll try and have coffee for you every morning."

"You don't have to do that," I objected.

"I want to," April insisted.

I didn't know what to say to that, so I just nodded.

April started to walk away, but then she stopped abruptly and turned back towards me. She stared straight into my eyes, and even in the dark I suddenly noticed that she had the same blue, big, and solemn eyes that June had.

"Why did you kill those men last night?" She asked with a soft voice.

I was startled by the question, and several seconds passed as I thought on that.

"It seemed like the thing to do," I finally replied.

"Did you enjoy it?"

"Not particularly."

"But you seemed so eager."

"Fast is how I would describe it."

April bit her lip as she thought on that.

"If there had been another way, would you have still killed them?"

"There is no other way with men like that."

"But you could have been killed," April said, and she suddenly looked worried.

"Possible," I agreed. "But not likely."

59

"They didn't seem to know that," April objected. "They seemed quite confident."

"They weren't confident. They were ignorant," I corrected. "And being ignorant can be costly."

April pinched her face in thought. Several seconds passed before she changed the subject.

"I heard Yancy Landon talking about you once, back in Midway."

"All good things, I'm sure," I smiled.

"He said you were an outlaw."

"I've been called that, yes."

"But you're not like those men last night."

"No, ma'am."

"What makes you so different?"

I smiled faintly.

"I'm not sure. But I'm different, I can assure you that."

April cocked her head sideways and smiled at me.

"Yes, I think you're different too."

I grinned and took a swig of coffee.

"I'm sorry for bothering you with all my questions," April said. "I'm just curious."

"Not at all," I replied. "I enjoy talking with you."

"I enjoy it too," she said. It was silent, and she added hesitantly, "June really likes you."

I was startled.

"She likes me?"

"She does. But, she's also scared of you."

"What for?"

"She saw you kill those men."

I frowned distastefully.

"She saw that?"

April nodded.

"She was upstairs, in the hallway."

"I'm sorry," I said.

"It wasn't your fault," April replied, and added, "She'll get over it. Sadly, she's seen death before."

60

A pained expression crossed April's face as she remembered the past. I didn't know what to say, so I just sat there.

"Well, I'd better get busy," April said abruptly. She smiled at me once more and walked towards the kitchen.

"Thanks for the coffee," I said.

Chapter fourteen

Brian joined me right as it was getting daylight. April served us breakfast, and afterwards we drank some more coffee. The only person in the room besides us was April, and she was behind the bar.

Amos suddenly burst into the hotel, looking excited.

"Ike Nash just rode into town," he announced. "He's got men with him."

"How many?" I asked.

"Four. They're coming this way."

April looked worried while I frowned thoughtfully.

"Amos, go find Ross," I said.

"I just saw him at the jail," Amos said.

I scowled at him.

"Well, go get him!"

Amos looked startled.

"Oh. Yes, sir. I'm sorry," he stammered and hurried out the door.

I looked at Brian and frowned.

"There he goes, apologizing again."

Brian smiled and shrugged in response.

"There's a shotgun behind the bar," I told him. "Grab it, and sit down over there across the room."

"Shotgun can be messy," Brian objected.

"Sure can," I agreed, and then I looked at April. "Where's June?"

"She's upstairs, still asleep."

"Good," I nodded. "Any shooting starts, you dive into the kitchen and keep your head down."

April nodded. Brian grabbed the shotgun, and we both checked our weapons. Then, Brian walked across the room and sat at a table, and he positioned himself so that he could see the entire room.

It was silent as we waited. A few tense minutes passed, and we heard noises from outside.

Seconds later, Ike Nash walked in with four men. Butch Nelson was behind him, and he led the men to the bar while Ike walked over to my table.

"I'm Ike Nash," he declared in a loud, booming voice.

"Lee Mattingly."

"You know who I am?"

"I do," I nodded.

"I know who you are too."

"Most folks do," I smiled.

Ike grunted. He looked around the room, and his gaze fell on Brian. He studied the shotgun in Brian's hands, and a small smile crossed his face.

"Smart, spreading out like that."

"I thought so," I agreed.

"You know my man Brock?"

"We've met, yes."

"He says you're a smart man."

"He would know," I smiled.

Ike made a sarcastic sound, and it fell silent as he looked around some more. He nodded to himself as he studied our hotel.

"Very impressive," he said.

"Thank you."

"Did you build the place yourself?"

"No. A saw and hammer never did fit right in my hand," I replied. "I mainly supervised."

Ike smiled and gestured at a chair.

"May I sit?"

"Go ahead."

Ike eased into a chair across the table from me.

"We need to talk," he said.

"About what?"

"You killed two of my men last night."

"I did," I confirmed.

"Why? They were just looking for a good time, is all."

"They were looking in the wrong place," I said, and Ike frowned at me.

"I can't afford for my men to be shot to doll rags every time they come to town," he objected.

"I can see how you'd feel that way," I nodded.

"So we need to reach an agreement of some sort."

"I've always been agreeable."

"Do you have any suggestions?"

I thought for a moment.

"All I ask is that your men behave themselves and don't harass my customers."

"And if they don't?"

"Then I'll shoot them," I declared, and nodded at Brian. "Or, he will."

"That's your idea of an agreement?" Ike scowled.

"Sure."

"That doesn't sound very legal to me."

"Nobody's perfect," I shrugged.

Ike sat silently for a moment, looking at me thoughtfully.

There was a noise at the door, and Ross walked in. He studied the men at the bar, and then he spotted Brian. He glanced at us, moved to the other corner of the room, and sat down.

"This lifestyle doesn't fit you," Ike spoke back up. "You're not a businessman. You belong outdoors."

"What I am," I replied slowly, "is none of your business."

Ike grunted and leaned forward in his chair.

"I want to buy this hotel," he announced boldly.

I shook my head.

"This hotel isn't for sale."

"Name your price," Ike said as he ignored my comment.

I shook my head again.

64

"I'll pay you twice what it's worth," Ike tried again. "And, after I buy the place you and Brian can work for me. I'll pay you top wages."

"No thanks."

Ike didn't seem bothered or upset. Instead, he just nodded as he stood.

"All right then, I'm not one to beg. You'll be sorry you didn't accept my offer."

"Perhaps."

"I'll talk with my men. They won't cause you anymore trouble."

"I appreciate that."

Ike nodded. He looked at Brian once more, and then he turned and walked proudly out of the hotel. His men followed after him.

Chapter fifteen

Ross and Brian walked over to my table.

"What was that all about?" Ross asked.

"I'm not exactly sure," I replied.

"Besides buying the hotel, what else did he want?"

"He asked me to stop killing people."

"What'd you say to that?"

"I told him I'd only shoot those that deserve it."

"And he went along with that?" Ross smiled faintly.

"We'll find out."

Ross's smile disappeared, and he suddenly looked worried.

"I wish Rondo would get back," he said wistfully, and asked, "Do you need me for anything else?"

"No," I replied. "Thanks for dropping by."

"Anytime," Ross replied, and then he left.

***

We opened up for breakfast about an hour later. The lobby became crowded, and all of the tables were full.

I sat at our corner table. I trimmed and lit a cigar, and I leaned back and watched the activity.

There was a hum of chatter in the room, and our waiters hustled about. April was busy cleaning dirty tables, and Amos was behind the bar.

I spotted June coming down the stairs, still dressed in her nightgown. She looked around the room, and she headed straight for my table as soon as she spotted me.

"Good morning, Mister Lee," she said, and she pulled up a chair and sat close beside me.

I was taken back by her boldness, but I recovered quickly.

"June," I said. "Did you sleep well?"

66

"Somebody kept snoring in the room next to us."

"That was probably Brian," I smiled.

She nodded, and it fell silent. A few minutes passed, and April spotted her. She frowned and hurried over.

"June," she scolded. "I told you to stay upstairs."

"But I'm hungry," June objected.

April started to respond, but I spoke up before she could.

"Go ahead and feed her breakfast," I said.

"Are you sure?"

I nodded, and a grateful look crossed April's face.

"Thank you," she said, and then she hurried away.

She returned a few minutes later. She placed a plate of food in front of June, and she tore into the meal with a vengeance.

"Don't eat so fast," April scolded, and then she returned to the kitchen.

I watched June eat with an amused smile. Several minutes passed, and then I cleared my throat.

"June," I said. "I'm sorry you saw that last night."

"Saw what?"

"Saw me kill those two men."

"Oh."

"Did you and your Ma talk about it?"

"Some. Ma said they were bad men," June said between bites.

"That's right. They were."

"Then why are you sorry?"

"I'm not sorry I did it; I'm just sorry you saw it," I explained.

"Why?"

I scratched my jaw as I pondered that.

"Well, a girl your age shouldn't see things like that," I finally said.

June nodded. I studied her, hoping to see signs of understanding, but she looked unconcerned as she continued eating.

67

"Anyway, I just thought you should know that," I finally said.

"Mister Lee," June said suddenly, and she looked up at me through those big, blue eyes.

"Yes?"

"I think my Ma likes you."

I was startled, and I almost dropped my cigar. I recovered, and then I just stared at her.

"What do you mean? She likes me as a friend?"

"I don't know; she just likes you," June shrugged, and then she added, "Sometimes, when Ma thinks I'm asleep, she cries at night. She misses Pa and May. I do too."

A felt a tug on my heartstrings. I didn't know what to say to that, so I just nodded slowly.

June returned to her breakfast, and several minutes passed. I just sat there in stunned silence, thinking on what June had said.

"Mister Lee," June said after a while.

"Yes?" I asked, and I was almost fearful of what she'd say next.

"Your cigar sure does smell. Ma says it's a nasty habit."

Again, I was startled. I stared at her for several seconds, but she ignored me as she finished her breakfast.

I shook my head in wonder, and I sighed as I put out my cigar.

Chapter sixteen

Brock spotted Ike and his men returning from town. He walked up to the main house and waited as they dismounted.

"A man's here to see you, Boss," he said as he took Ike's horse. "He's waiting in your study."

"Oh? Who is it?"

"Says his name is Jeremiah Wisdom."

"That's the gambler we sent for," Butch spoke up.

Ike nodded and turned towards the house. Meanwhile, Butch tied his horse to the hitching post and followed after him.

"Don't go anywhere," Ike told Brock. "I'll need to see you later."

Brock nodded. He watched as Ike and Butch disappeared inside, and then he led Ike's horse down to the barn.

***

Jeremiah Wisdom stood as Ike and Butch entered the study.

"I'm sorry to keep you waiting," Ike said as he walked forward. "I had other business to take care of."

"Don't worry about it," Jeremiah replied, and they shook hands.

Jeremiah was in his mid-thirties. An educated man, he was cunning and careful. He was tall and thin, and his face was dark from the sun. He also spoke Apache fluently and wore a Colt on his hip.

Ike sat behind his desk while Butch went to his corner. Jeremiah sat back down, and it was silent as Ike studied him.

"You don't look like a gambler," Ike finally said. "You look more like a cowpuncher."

69

"I don't consider myself to be a gambler, so I'll take that as a compliment," Jeremiah said.

"Oh?" Ike looked disappointed. "We heard you were an exceptional poker player. That's why we sent for you."

"Just because I'm not a gambler doesn't mean I'm not a clever poker player," Jeremiah corrected.

"So you can play?"

"I can."

"And you're good?"

"I don't lose," Jeremiah declared matter-of-factly.

Ike smiled and nodded.

"You rode with Wade Davis," Ike recalled.

"That's right."

"Why did you leave him?"

Jeremiah paused as he collected his thoughts.

"I learned a long time ago to never hate your enemies," he explained. "It affects your judgment. I tried to tell Wade that, but he wouldn't listen."

"And it got him killed," Ike said.

"It sure did."

Ike liked that. He glanced at Butch and looked back at Jeremiah.

"Are you any good with that?" He gestured at Jeremiah's Colt.

"Yes."

"How good, exactly?"

Jeremiah pinched his face in thought.

"Well, I have the respect of Yancy Landon."

Ike looked intrigued.

"How do you know that?"

"He told me once, a long time ago."

"I wasn't aware that you knew the Landons."

"I get around."

"How about Lee Mattingly?"

"We've met."

"Anything personal between you two?"

"No."

Ike nodded and leaned forward in his chair.

"You're probably wondering why I sent for you."

"I figured you'd get around to it, sooner or later."

"I have a plan," Ike announced, and then he carefully explained all the details.

Afterwards, it was silent as Jeremiah thought on it, and Ike waited patiently.

"It's a good plan," Jeremiah finally said.

"So you'll agree to do it?"

"You forgot to mention the pay."

"Name your price," Ike shrugged.

Jeremiah did, and Ike agreed. Afterwards, Jeremiah nodded and stood.

"It's settled then. Now, if you'll excuse me, I'd like to rest up a bit."

"Of course," Ike nodded. "Butch, show Jeremiah to the guest room, and then tell Brock I need to see him. After that, you'd better ride back to town and tell Amos it's time."

"I'll take care of it," Butch said, and he and Jeremiah left the study.

Chapter seventeen

Our second day of business was much better than the first.

None of Ike's hands showed up. The restaurant and gaming tables stayed busy, and I even won at poker.

Brian and I were up early the next morning. We dressed, splashed some water in our faces, and went downstairs and sat at our usual table.

April was already in the kitchen. She served us breakfast and coffee, and I smiled at her.

"Thank you, April."

"You're welcome, Lee," she flashed a smile back.

April stood there a moment. She looked like she wanted to say something else, but she changed her mind and returned to the kitchen.

Brian looked thoughtful. He shot me a quizzical look, but didn't say anything.

It was silent while we ate. A few minutes passed, and April reappeared with a broom. She started sweeping the floor, and I watched her with a curious look.

Brian looked up from his breakfast and spotted me watching her.

"What are you looking at?"

"I was just thinking," I said wistfully.

"About what?"

"Jessica."

Brian scowled at me.

"So you're staring at Mrs. Gibson, but thinking about Jessica?"

"I wasn't staring," I objected.

"That's what it looked like to me."

"It suddenly occurred to me that I can't remember what Jessica looks like," I said as I ignored Brian's comment.

"Are you feeling all right?" Brian looked at me oddly.

"For some reason I can't picture her face," I said as I continued to ignore his comments. "Does that ever happen to you?"

"Half the time, I can't even remember what *I* look like."

I chuckled, and we finished our breakfast.

We were almost through when June came down the stairs. Her hair was a mess, and she was still in her nightgown. She looked groggy as she walked to our table and sat beside me.

"Morning, June," I smiled at her.

"Hi, Mister Lee," June said as she rubbed her eyes.

"You're up early this morning," I commented. "Are you hungry?"

June nodded sleepily.

"April," I called out. "We have another guest for breakfast."

April stopped sweeping, and she frowned when she spotted her daughter.

"June, I told you not to bother Mister Lee," she scolded.

"She's not bothering anybody," I spoke up.

A grateful look crossed April's face.

"Thank you," she said. "Thank you very much."

I smiled and nodded. Meanwhile, an anxious look suddenly crossed June's face.

"I gotta go," she announced. "I gotta go now."

April started towards our table, but I stood and waved my hand at her.

"Go get her breakfast," I said. "I'll take her."

"Are you sure?"

"Go on," I said.

April flashed me a smile as she hurried to the kitchen. Meanwhile, I took June by the hand and headed towards the back door.

Brian never said a word. He just sat there and watched us with a thoughtful look.

73

Chapter eighteen

Lady luck finally remembered me.

For the second night in a row, I was actually winning at poker. There was more money than usual in the game, and the pots were big.

It didn't take me long to accumulate a big pile of cash. The night was still young, and I was eager for more.

I won a few more hands, and then everybody decided to take a break. I didn't want to stop playing, but I had no choice.

Some of the players went outside to visit the outhouse while others went for coffee.

April usually brought me coffee during breaks, so I remained seated and waited patiently. I organized my pile of cash, and then I trimmed and lit a cigar.

I took a puff, and as I exhaled a stranger walked into the room.

I narrowed my eyes as I studied him. He was tall, thin, and had a dark, tanned face. I had seen him before, but I couldn't remember where.

He walked up to the table. He pulled out a wad of bills so thick it could have choked a cow, and then he smiled at me.

"Can I join?"

"Sit down," I said as I eyed all that cash.

He nodded and sat across from me, and it was then that I recalled who he was.

"You're Jeremiah Wisdom."

"That's right," he nodded. "And you'd be Lee Mattingly."

"You used to run around with the Landons," I recollected.

"And you used to run *from* the Landons."

I smiled at that.

74

"Weren't you with Wade Davis earlier this year?" I asked.

"I was, but he's dead now. The Landons killed him."

"I remember that," I nodded, and added, "I hear you're a good poker player."

"Let's find out, shall we?" Jeremiah smiled.

"Yes, let's," I smiled back.

Other players started drifting back. April appeared from the kitchen, carrying a coffee pot and a few cups.

Jeremiah spotted her, and his eyes lit up with interest. He smiled and stood as she arrived at our table.

"Good evening, ma'am," he said.

April smiled politely and glanced at me.

"I brought you some coffee."

"Thank you, April."

She poured me a cup and glanced at Jeremiah.

"Would you like some?"

"I sure would," Jeremiah said eagerly.

April poured another cup and turned to leave.

"Thank you, ma'am," Jeremiah said.

April nodded. She glanced at me and smiled warmly, and then she walked back towards the kitchen.

Jeremiah remained standing as he watched her. Soon as she was gone, he smiled wistfully and sat. Meanwhile, I frowned disapprovingly.

"She seems like a nice lady," he commented innocently.

"She is."

"Do you know her well?"

"Some."

Jeremiah looked thoughtful, but he didn't say anything else.

By now everyone else had returned. They sat around the table, and the game started.

Chapter nineteen

A little voice inside me told me to be careful. But I was suddenly feeling irritable, and I ignored the warning.

I bet big and won the first hand, and I won again a few hands later. My confidence soared, and I felt unbeatable.

If I had been paying attention, I would have noticed that Jeremiah wasn't winning. Instead, he let everyone else win while he learned our bad habits.

The game changed drastically about an hour later.

By now I had more than doubled my pile of cash, and I was playing dangerously. But then, as if someone slammed a door, all of a sudden I couldn't win a hand to save my life. The pots started getting higher, and Jeremiah started winning.

I should have seen what was happening, but instead I became even more overconfident and arrogant.

Have you ever seen a fisherman set a hook? That's what Jeremiah did to me. He put the bait out there, I nibbled, and he yanked hard and sunk the hook deep in my jaw.

I was getting desperate when the best hand of the night was finally dealt to me. I couldn't believe my luck. I held three kings and two jacks, meaning a full house. My palms got sweaty in anticipation.

I should have been wary, because Jeremiah was dealing. But I was desperate to recover what I'd lost, so once again I ignored that little voice inside me.

It was my bet. I looked at my cards once more, and then I eyed the cash that I had remaining on the table.

"I have around two thousand here," I said, and I pushed it all towards the middle of the table.

A surprised murmur went around the table.

"Too rich for me," the man next to me said, and one by one everybody folded until the bet came to Jeremiah.

Jeremiah took in a big breath and let it out slowly. He looked at his cards once more and smiled.

"Why not," he said.

It was silent as he counted his money. Then, he reached inside his vest pocket and pulled out another wad of cash.

Jeremiah looked at me.

"I'll call your two thousand, and I raise you eight thousand."

There was a surprised hum in the room, followed by a tense silence. I hadn't noticed before, but Brian stood in the corner, and he was watching closely.

All eyes were on me. I looked at my cards once more and frowned thoughtfully.

"I'll call," I said, and my voice was hoarse.

"I don't see any money on the table."

"We can cover it," I said. "The money's in the safe in my office."

A few seconds passed as Jeremiah thought on that, and then he nodded.

"Fine by me," he said, and asked, "How many cards?"

"I'll play these."

"Dealer takes two," he said.

He discarded two cards and dealt himself two more. His movements were slow and deliberate, and all eyes were on him.

I watched him closely as he picked up his cards, but his face remained emotionless.

"Your bet," he said.

"Check."

"Check," Jeremiah nodded.

I took in another big breath. I glanced at Brian, and his face was pale.

It was time. My hands trembled as I placed my cards on the table.

"Full house," I announced, and an excited murmur went through the crowd.

77

Jeremiah showed no emotion. A few long seconds passed, and one by one he placed his cards down on the table.

"Four aces," he said softly.

Loud cheers and applause sounded out, and Jeremiah grinned.

I felt like I'd just been kicked in the head by a mule. I couldn't breath, and all I could do was stare numbly at the cards.

"Lord help us," I heard Brian say.

Chapter twenty

Everyone congratulated Jeremiah and wanted to shake his hand. The celebration carried on and on while I just sat there with a pained expression.

The crowd finally thinned. Jeremiah glanced at me and smiled pleasantly.

"Can we talk? Somewhere private?"

I swallowed and licked my lips.

"In my office," I managed.

I stood and walked toward the stairs. Jeremiah grabbed all the money on the table and followed after me.

Brian joined us in the office, and his face was dark. He walked over to the window and looked out into the black night.

I sat behind the desk, and I still displayed a stunned look on my face. Meanwhile, Jeremiah dropped all of the money onto the table, and then he sat in a chair across the desk, looking pleased.

"I reckon we should count it and see how much money is there," Jeremiah suggested.

"I reckon we should," I said flatly.

"I'll do it," Brian offered.

Nobody said anything as Brian walked over to the desk, and it was silent as he counted. After he was done, he neatly arranged all the bills into several tall stacks.

"Mr. Wisdom, we owe you ten thousand and fifty-two dollars," Brian announced.

"Please, call me Jeremiah," he said, and added, "I like round numbers. Let's just make it an even ten thousand, shall we?"

"It's your money," Brian said.

"A man could get killed carrying that much cash around," Jeremiah figured.

"It's happened before," Brian agreed.

"Not only do I have your ten thousand, but I also have ten thousand of my own. That's twenty thousand."

"You're a rich man," Brian sounded tired.

"That safe you mentioned. Could I leave all twenty thousand there and pick it up in the morning?"

"That would be fine."

"Good," Jeremiah smiled and stood. "I'd also like a room."

"See Amos at the bar," Brian instructed. "He'll get you settled."

"How much for the room?"

"No charge. You're our guest."

Jeremiah nodded and turned to go.

"Thank you. I'll see you in the morning."

Brian managed to mumble something as Jeremiah left.

We didn't speak as Brian opened the safe and put Jeremiah's money in. It was too painful to watch, so I grabbed a cigar, trimmed it and lit it, and then took a long, deep puff.

"Do we have ten thousand to cover it?" I finally broke the silence.

"We're a little short," Brian replied quietly.

"Tomorrow's payday too, ain't it."

"It is."

I sighed and leaned back in my chair.

"What'll we do?"

"Only thing we *can* do is to go to the bank in the morning and get a loan. We don't need much. Just enough to cover everything for a week or so."

"Don't forget about Mr. Tomlin's steers," I reminded. "We haven't paid him yet."

"I'll borrow enough for that too."

"What a mess," I sighed.

"That about describes it."

"I'm sorry, Brian."

He shrugged.

"If I was you, I'd have done the same thing. When you put that full house down on the table I thought you'd won for sure."

"It was a nice feeling, if only for a brief moment," I recalled.

"Do you think he cheated?"

"I have my suspicions."

"But suspicion ain't proof," Brian pointed out.

"I know," I muttered. It was silent, and I added, "Well, things can't get any worse."

"You said that once already."

"I did, didn't I," I admitted.

Brian nodded and moved towards the door. I stood, put out my cigar, and followed after him.

"Things will be better tomorrow," I said as we walked into the lobby.

Brian grunted in response.

Chapter twenty-one

We turned in early.

It only took Brian a few minutes to start snoring, but I tossed and turned.

I kept replaying the hand over and over in my mind, and I finally came to the conclusion that Jeremiah had cheated. Problem was, I didn't know how. I had watched him deal those last two cards off the top of the deck, clear as day.

I was still thinking about that when I heard a faint noise from downstairs. I sat up in bed and listened. A few seconds passed, and I heard something again.

I crawled out of bed and pulled my pants on. Next, I grabbed my Colt, eased the door open, and stepped out into the hallway.

I looked down into the lobby, but it was pitch black and I couldn't see a thing.

I heard a noise again, over by the main door, and it sounded like somebody was opening the outer oak doors.

With my Colt in hand, I walked down the hallway and eased down the stairs. The boards creaked underneath my feet, and I winced.

I could see a silhouette of someone standing in the doorway. The person was tall and wide, and he had his back to me. I wasn't sure, but it looked like Brock.

Being as quiet as possible, I left the stairs and walked towards him.

I heard another noise. This time it was behind me, and I started to spin around. But, before I could, strong hands grabbed me and threw me forward.

With a surprised grimace, I landed in the middle of a table. It shattered, and my flailing arms knocked over a chair. The impact caused me to drop my Colt, and I heard it hit the floor.

I was tangled up in the splintered table. I tried to stand, but then those same strong hands grabbed ahold of me again. I was spun around, and a hard fist greeted me in the face.

I staggered backwards, and as I did I attempted a roundhouse swing. But, the huge form in front of me easily blocked my ineffective blow. He lashed out again, and I tasted blood as I went flying backwards.

I landed in a heap and was knocked senseless. I gasped as I tried to recover, but then my attacker viciously kicked me in my midsection.

I groaned and curled into a compulsory ball. The breath was knocked out of me, and I couldn't move.

I saw a pair of boots standing in front of me. Seconds later, I felt a hard blow on the back of my head.

Lights exploded. I managed to groan, and then darkness closed in around me as I passed out.

Chapter twenty-two

"Easy now. He's waking up."

My head hurt, my back hurt, everything hurt. I groaned as I forced my eyes open.

I blinked my eyes several times before things finally came into focus.

I was still on the floor in the lobby, and several lanterns had been lit. April and Brian were knelt beside me, and Ross stood behind them.

June stood over by the stairs in her nightgown, and her eyes were wide with fright.

April looked concerned. She had a wet towel, and she was wiping blood from my head. I could already feel a huge knot on the back of my head, and it was painful.

"What happened?" She asked.

I swallowed and licked my lips.

"A fight," I managed. "I lost."

"I can see that," she smiled.

"What time is it?" I asked hoarsely.

"'Bout an hour before daylight," Brian explained. "April came down and found you. She woke me, and I sent her after Ross."

I frowned thoughtfully.

"I've been down here a while then."

"What happened?" Ross spoke up.

"I heard a noise over by the door," I explained. "I came downstairs, and somebody jumped me from behind. I think he came from the office."

A worried look crossed Brian's face. He stood, grabbed a lantern, and hurried into the office. He returned a few seconds later looking grim.

"Did you recognize them?" He asked.

I had my suspicions, but I didn't want to say too much in front of Ross.

84

"It was dark," I said instead.

"Well, whoever it was, they broke into our safe," Brian muttered. "They took it all."

"All?"

"Yes, all."

Several stunned seconds passed, and I groaned softly.

I heard a muffled chuckle. I glanced up and saw Ross trying to hide a smile.

"What's so funny?" I glared at him.

"I'm sorry, but I can't help but think how ironic this situation is."

"How so?"

"You two used to make a living by stealing from others, and now it's happened to you. A switch of fortunes, so to speak."

A surge of anger passed through me, and I fought to control my emotions.

"Ross," I said.

"Yes, Lee?"

"You can leave now."

Ross stared at me, and he narrowed his eyes when he saw how serious I was.

"Sure," he said. "Soon as it gets daylight, I'll ride out and look for tracks."

"I'll go with you," Brian offered.

Ross nodded. He glanced at me once more, and then he left.

"Let's get you up," April suggested.

I nodded. April and Brian both offered a hand, and they helped pull me up.

I was dizzy. I swayed a bit, but then April grabbed me.

Even though I was in considerable pain, I couldn't help but noticed how fresh and clean April smelled. I put my arm around her shoulder as we walked towards the stairs.

"Let's get you to your bed, and then I'll bring you some breakfast," she said.

"Thank you, April."

We passed by June, and she was still staring at me through wide eyes.

"Mister Lee," June said in her soft and timid voice.

"Yes, June?"

"You look awful."

"Go back to bed, June."

"Yes, sir, Mister Lee."

Chapter twenty-three

A few minutes later I was in bed on my back, with a pillow propped behind my aching head. April had gone downstairs to fix my breakfast, and Brian was standing in the corner, looking broodily out the window.

"I thought you said things would be better today," he grumbled.

"I guess I lied."

"We're in big trouble now."

"Really? I didn't know."

"There's no way we can borrow enough money to pay Jeremiah," Brian said as he ignored my sarcastic comment.

"What will we do then?"

Brian frowned thoughtfully.

"We'll explain what happened, and then ask Jeremiah for some time. This hotel is making money. All we need is some time. A lot of time."

"How 'bout payroll?"

"I can borrow enough for that and Mr. Tomlin's steers."

I thought it over and nodded. Meanwhile, Brian turned from the window and looked at me.

"Now that we're alone, do you know who it was?"

"Brock and Amos," I declared.

"You're sure?"

"Not entirely," I admitted. "It happened so fast. But it was Amos that attacked me, and the guy's shadow in the door looked like Brock."

"How can you see a shadow in the dark?" Brian looked at me oddly.

"You know what I mean," I scowled.

"Is that all you can remember?"

"No. The feller that attacked me was wearing boots."

"What did these boots look like?" Brian looked hopeful.

"They were just plain-looking boots. Nothing special that I can remember."

"Well, that really narrows it down," Brian said sourly.

I shrugged and then winced as a sharp pain pounded my head.

"Amos hasn't come in yet," Brian commented as he looked back out the window.

"Act normal when he does," I said. "I want to see how guilty he acts."

Brian nodded, and it was silent for several minutes.

"You want to know the one thing that really bothers me?" I said after a while.

"Just one?"

"Out of all the men I've killed over years, not once did I attack from behind. They all saw it coming."

"Well, at least you *heard* it coming."

"Amos is going to pay for this," I vowed.

"If it was him," Brian reminded.

"It was him," I muttered.

"Well, I'd better go saddle my horse," Brian said as he moved towards the door. "We'll talk to Jeremiah when I get back."

I nodded, and Brian walked out the door.

Chapter twenty-four

April brought my breakfast to my room. It was now daylight, and she gasped when she saw my face.

"Oh my," she said. "You look like a raccoon."

"Thanks."

"How do you feel?"

"Probably how I look."

"I'm sorry," she said.

I grunted. I took a swig of coffee and winced as I swallowed.

April stood silently in front of me. I glanced up, and those big, blue eyes were staring at me solemnly.

"June is really worried about you," she said.

"Tell her I'll be fine."

"I will," April nodded. She hesitated, and added, "June has become quite fond of you. So have I."

I was startled and didn't know what to say.

"I – I mean - we would be devastated if anything were to happen to you. I'm not sure if June could take it. She's already lost so much."

"Nobody's killed me yet."

"But there's trouble coming, isn't there?"

"Yes, I think there is."

"You will be careful, won't you?"

"Sure."

April didn't look convinced as she walked towards the door.

"I'll leave you alone so you can get some rest," she said.

"Thanks for the breakfast, April. I really appreciate it."

"Of course," she smiled at me, and added, "I'm sorry you lost the, uh, boxing match."

"It wasn't boxing," I grumbled. "It was more like bare knuckled fist fighting."

"What's the difference?"

89

"Rules," I grumbled.

***

After breakfast I dressed in some fresh clothes, splashed some water in my face, buckled my gun-belt on, and went downstairs. I was extremely sore, and my movements were slow.

The lobby was full of customers eating breakfast. I spotted Jeremiah sitting at the corner table, and he had a full plate in front of him.

Amos was at the other end of the bar, tending to a customer. He looked unconcerned as he went about his business.

"It was you," I muttered as I watched him.

I turned and went into the office, and neither Amos nor Jeremiah saw me.

I needed a cigar. I grabbed one from my desk, trimmed it carefully, lit it, and took a deep puff.

I sighed in contentment as I sat behind my desk and enjoyed my smoke. Afterwards, I stood painfully and studied the safe.

The safe looked untouched. In fact, there weren't even any scratch marks on it.

I was still at the safe when Brian walked in. He watched me a moment and cleared his throat.

"Feel any better?"

"No," I replied, and asked, "Find anything?"

"No. Ground was too hard."

"I figured as much."

"Amos showed up," Brian announced. "He's tending bar."

"I saw him."

"Has he confessed yet?"

"Surprisingly, no."

90

Brian nodded, and then he watched curiously as I opened the safe and studied the hinges.

"Looking for something?"

"A clue would be nice."

"Found one yet?"

"No," I grumbled, and asked, "How do you figure they got into the safe? There aren't even any scratch marks."

"Either they knew the combination or they picked it," Brian declared.

"Who knows the combination?"

"Just you and me."

I frowned. I started to reply, but before I could Jeremiah walked in looking jovial.

"Good morning!" He said.

Chapter twenty-five

Jeremiah's cheerful look disappeared when he saw my face.

"What happened to you?" He looked startled.

"I bumped into a table."

"That looks painful."

"It is."

"You should be more careful," he chided.

"Thanks for the advice," I said stiffly.

"So, what else happened?"

I didn't answer. I looked at Brian, and he stepped forward and cleared his throat.

"We were robbed last night," he announced.

Jeremiah looked genuinely concerned.

"What? Who did it?"

"We're not sure," Brian replied.

"What did they take?"

"They broke into the safe," Brian explained. "They took all our money, including yours."

A thoughtful look crossed Jeremiah's face. It was silent for several seconds, and he sat in the chair across the desk from me.

"I take it you caught them in the act?" He looked at me.

"I did," I nodded.

"Do you know who did it? Did you get a good look?"

"No. It was dark."

"So they got away."

"For now."

Jeremiah pinched his face in displeasure. I looked at Brian, and he cleared his throat again.

"We owe you twenty thousand dollars," Brian said.

"You most certainly do."

"And you'll get it, but it's going to take time," Brian said, and then he outlined our plan.

92

Jeremiah listened, and afterwards a heavy silence filled the room as he thought on that.

"What am I supposed to do while I'm waiting?" He finally asked sarcastically. "Sit in my room and twiddle my thumbs?"

Neither one of us replied.

"I want my money," Jeremiah declared. "I want it now."

"I'm sorry," I spoke, and my voice was husky. "But we don't have it."

"What about the hotel?"

"What about it?" I narrowed my eyes.

"You own it, don't you?"

"That would be correct, yes."

"It's simple then. I figure the hotel's worth about what you owe me. Sign it over, and we'll be even."

"No," I said firmly. "We won't do that."

"Any court of law would side with me," Jeremiah pointed out.

"You can't have the hotel," I said, and my voice was curt.

"I don't think you have a choice," Jeremiah replied calmly.

I felt a rage starting to build inside me. I sat up in my chair, and my knuckles turned white as I gripped the edge of my desk. Jeremiah however, didn't seem to be upset.

"Before things get ugly, I have a proposition that might make everybody happy," he said.

I took in a big breath and let it out slowly as I fought to control my emotions.

"Let's hear it," I said.

"Nothing would change much," Jeremiah said. "You two would still run the hotel as if you owned it. The only difference is that I would get twenty percent of the earnings. Then, when you can afford it, you can buy the hotel back and I'll be on my way. In the meantime, I want the deed to the hotel for security."

93

"That sounds reasonable," Brian spoke quickly, and then he looked at me. "What do you think, Lee?"

I didn't like it, and I frowned suspiciously as I studied Jeremiah's face. But he revealed nothing as he calmly returned my gaze.

I sighed and looked at Brian.

"Are you sure about this?"

"What else *can* we do?"

I didn't have a reply to that. With a deep frown, I looked back at Jeremiah and nodded slightly.

Jeremiah smiled and nodded graciously.

"I have one more suggestion," he said.

I was silent, so Brian asked, "Yes?"

"We all want the hotel to make money," he said. "Am I correct?"

"Just get to the point," I said sourly.

"Even though I'm now the owner, I still have nothing to do. So, I suggest that I take over the poker room. You'll make your money back faster if I play."

"Are you trying to insult me?" I leaned over the desk and thrust out my jaw.

"Of course not. I'll just let the truth speak for itself. You lost; I won. And, to make money you must win."

That burned. I couldn't think of an answer, and the silence was uncomfortable.

"Lee, it might not be a bad idea," Brian spoke up. "You look horrible. You could use a few days off anyway to rest up and recover."

I scowled at Brian but didn't say anything.

"It's settled then?" Jeremiah asked.

I remained silent, so Brian said, "Yes, it's settled."

"Good!" Jeremiah looked pleased. "Now, I want this agreement to be legal."

"I'll draw up the papers," Brian offered.

"That'll be fine," Jeremiah said, and he stood to leave. "I'll sign them tonight."

94

Brian nodded, and Jeremiah walked out the door.

"Are you all right?" Brian turned to me.

"No," I muttered. "I don't trust him."

"There weren't any other options to choose from, Lee. He had us."

"I know," I admitted, and asked, "What about Jessica?"

"What about her?"

"We just gave her hotel away."

"We'll get it back before she finds out," Brian declared.

I had my doubts, but I didn't say anything.

Chapter twenty-six

Jeremiah won big at poker that night, and the restaurant was full of customers. I wasn't needed, so I went upstairs and turned in early.

I was still sore and stiff the next morning. I splashed some water in my face, got dressed, strapped on my gun belt, and went downstairs.

I could hear a low hum of laughter and chatter. I was curious, but then my face turned dark as I walked into the lobby.

Jeremiah Wisdom sat at my corner table, eating breakfast. June was seated beside him, and they were teasing one another.

I tried to hide my displeasure as I walked over to them. They looked up, and June smiled at me.

"What are you doing up this early?" Jeremiah looked concerned.

"I'm an early riser," I replied curtly, and added, "I always eat my breakfast at this table."

"Sit down," he offered. "Join us."

"Thanks," I said stiffly.

Jeremiah was in the chair that I usually sat in, so I walked around the table and sat across from him.

I heard a noise from the kitchen, and April appeared with a coffee pot. She smiled when she spotted me.

"Do you feel any better this morning?" She asked as she poured me a cup of coffee.

"Yes," I lied. "Much better."

"Good, I'm happy to hear that," she said. "I'll be right back with your breakfast."

"Thank you, April."

I looked at Jeremiah. He was watching April as she left, and I didn't like the yearning look in his eyes.

"Did Brian give you the good news?" Jeremiah looked over at me.

"No."

"The hotel made more money last night than it's ever made," Jeremiah looked proud.

"That's wonderful," I said tonelessly.

"I thought you'd be pleased."

I forced a smile, and it fell silent. A few minutes passed, and April brought me my breakfast.

I was chewing my first bite when June looked up suddenly.

"I gotta go," she said.

"Gotta go where?" Jeremiah looked at her and smiled.

"She needs to go to the outhouse," I explained, and then I looked at June. "All right, let's go."

I started to stand, but Jeremiah jumped to his feet and waved a hand at me.

"I'll take her," he said. "You just sit there and rest. Eat your breakfast."

I started to object, but he grabbed June's hand and took off before I could.

My face turned dark as I watched them.

Chapter twenty-seven

Brian Clark was successful in his attempt to get a loan, and we were able to cover our expenses.

Things went smoothly for two days. I recovered from my beating, and most of the soreness worked its way out. I still had a few bruises, but other than that I was fine.

The restaurant stayed full, and Jeremiah won at poker. I had a talk with him about playing honest, and he assured me he would.

Amos avoided me as much as possible, but that was nothing new. Other than that, he acted normal.

I was still convinced that it was him and Brock that robbed us. Problem was, I didn't know how to prove it.

Jeremiah disappeared after breakfast on the third day, and Amos didn't show up either. We didn't think much of it at first, but by midafternoon we started getting suspicious.

By now the lunch customers had left, and the place was mostly empty. Brian and I stood in front of the bar, and April was behind it.

There was a noise at the door. We turned and looked, and Ike Nash walked in looking important. Behind him trailed four of his hands, including Butch, and Jeremiah Wisdom was next. Ross Stewart brought up the rear, and he looked uncomfortable.

I narrowed my eyes. I stepped away from the bar and met them in the middle of the room.

"What is this?" I asked, and my voice was low and stern.

"I don't want any trouble," Ike said, and his booming voice filled the room. "I stopped at the jail and explained the situation to Ross, and I asked him to come along to keep things peaceful."

"What situation?"

Ike smiled pleasantly.

"I am now the owner of The Palace Hotel," he declared.

"No," I said flatly. "You're not."

Jeremiah cleared his throat. We all looked at him, and he shifted his feet timidly.

"I'm sorry, Lee, but Mr. Nash approached me and offered to buy the place. I know we had a deal, but Ike offered me double what the hotel's worth. What was I supposed to do?"

Ike smiled smugly, and I felt like I'd just been kicked in the head by a mule. I glanced at Brian, and he looked just as stunned. I also saw April behind the bar, and she was watching me with wide eyes.

I looked over at Ross, and he cleared his throat and stepped forward.

"I'm sorry, Lee," he said. "There's nothing I can do. You and Brian gave the hotel to Jeremiah to cover your debts, and Jeremiah has now sold the hotel to Mr. Nash. No matter how you look at it, Ike is now the legal owner."

For some reason, I couldn't talk. In a mere matter of seconds, I felt drained of life.

"I want everybody to hear this so there's no misunderstanding," Ike spoke up. "As the owner, I'm hiring Jeremiah Wisdom to run the hotel. He'll work for me from here on out. As for you and Brian-," he turned towards me, "I want both of you out of my hotel. I told Ross that, and he's going to stay here while you two get your belongings gathered."

A feeling of rage came over me, and I was tempted to kill Ike where he stood.

"You'll have to do as he says, Lee," Ross spoke quietly.

I ignored Ross as I glared at Ike.

I was about to make a grab for my Colt when, behind Ike, Jessica Tussle walked through the swinging doors.

99

Chapter twenty-eight

To say I was shocked was an understatement. My breath left me, and all I could do was stare at her.

"Lord help us," I heard Brian say softly.

Jessica wore a fancy, blue dress, and she carried a small suitcase. She looked fresh, clean, and beautiful.

She paused at the doorway. She took a slow look around the lobby, and she looked pleased.

She spotted us, and a big grin appeared on her face as she walked over.

Ike turned, and his face sharpened in curiosity. But Jessica didn't seem to notice him as she walked to me.

"Hello, Lee," she said, and her eyes twinkled.

"Jessica," I said stiffly. "What are you doing here?"

"Tussle had some business to attend too here in town, and I convinced him to bring me along. We just arrived on the stage," she said, and her face looked flushed and excited. "Lee, the hotel looks wonderful!"

I managed to nod. She glanced around at everyone, and she suddenly noticed all the somber looks.

"I'm sorry," she said. "Am I interrupting something?"

Ike saw an opportunity, and he stepped forward.

"My name is Ike Nash," he said pleasantly. "How do you do, ma'am?"

Jessica gave a small curtsy.

"I'm fine, thank you," she replied. "My name is Jessica Tussle."

"The pleasure is all mine," Ike grinned.

Jessica smiled politely and asked, "Are you a guest at the hotel?"

"No, ma'am," Ike beamed. "I'm the owner."

I made a small groaning sound.

Jessica didn't believe him, and she smiled coyly.

"Oh? I thought Lee and Brian were the owners."

"They were, but they're not anymore," Ike explained. "In fact, they were just leaving."

The playful look left Jessica's face. She frowned and looked at me.

"Is that true?"

I felt miserable. I swallowed hard and nodded.

Jessica's eyes turned hard and cold. She glared at me for several tense seconds, and I just stood there and took it.

"That is very interesting," she finally said.

"Would you like a room?" Ike asked. "I'd be honored if you'd be my guest."

Jessica took her eyes off me and looked back at Ike.

"No, thank you," she said curtly. "I'll make other arrangements."

Ike didn't like being rejected, and his face stiffened. He nodded and stepped back.

Meanwhile, Jessica turned her eyes back to me, and her gaze was fierce.

Several long, uncomfortable seconds passed. Then, without a word, she turned and walked briskly towards the door.

My heart broke as I watched her.

Chapter twenty-nine

Brian headed towards the stairs as soon as Jessica left, but I wasn't ready to leave.

I had just been humiliated, and I wanted to remember this moment and how it felt. I stood there silently and studied each one in the room.

My gaze finally came to Ike. I stared at him with an emotionless face, and he stared back.

Finally, Ike said, "Before you go, I'd be interested to know your plans."

"Haven't got any."

"Well, that'll be fine for a day or two while you get your affairs in order," Ike said. "But after that, I think it would be best if you two drifted on. We don't want any trouble."

"We'll keep that in mind."

It fell silent again as Ike and I continued to stare at each other. A long minute passed. Then I nodded to myself, turned, and walked towards the stairs.

***

Brian and I didn't talk as we packed our belongings.

From our window in our room, I watched as Ike and his men left town. Jeremiah wasn't with them, so I figured he was downstairs.

Ross was also downstairs, waiting on us. But we didn't care, and we took our time.

We finished packing, and then we heard a knock at the door.

"Yes?" I called out, and my hand gripped the handle of my Colt.

"It's me, April."

I released my grip on my Colt.

"Come on in, April."

April and June entered the room. Both of them looked worried, and June stared at me through those big, solemn eyes.

"Where are you two going?" April asked.

"We're not sure, exactly."

"What will you do now?"

I didn't have an answer, so I just shrugged.

"I'm so sorry about all this," April said. "I feel horrible."

"Don't," I said. "It's not your fault."

"Are you two leaving town?" April asked, and June's eyes grew wide.

"Yes, but we'll be around."

"What about me and June? Do I still have a job?"

"I'll talk with Jeremiah," I said. "You'll keep your job, I promise you."

"I don't want to cause any trouble."

"No trouble. I'd consider it a pleasure."

It was silent then, and April and I looked at each other. I could tell that she wanted to say something else, but she decided not to.

Finally, I cleared my throat.

"We've got to go," I said, and my voice was hoarse.

April nodded and bit her lip.

"I hope you come see us sometime," she said.

I nodded curtly. I grabbed my pack, and Brian and I headed towards the door.

For some reason I had a lump in my throat, and all I wanted was to get away as quickly as possible.

I reached the door, and I made the mistake of looking back. June was watching me and trying not to cry.

"Mister Lee," she said, and her voice was barely hearable.

"Yes?"

"Please don't go."

I took in a big breath and let it out slowly.

"Mind your Ma, June," I said, and then I walked out the door.

Chapter thirty

Ike Nash was in a good mood as they trotted back to the ranch.

"Well, that went well," he said.

"It did," Butch agreed, and added, "Lee sure looked mad."

"He did," Ike chuckled gruffly.

"Do you think he'll retaliate?"

"It's possible," Ike said. "But, the law's on our side. Anything they attempt will just make them look worse."

"I don't think that'll matter to Lee," Butch warned.

"They'd be foolish to try anything," Ike reasoned. "There's only two of them, and I've got over thirty men."

"What about Brock? There could be trouble if he bumped into Lee. They don't like each other."

"Brock won't be here," Ike replied.

"He won't?" Butch looked surprised.

"It's almost time for him to meet the Gant brothers," Ike explained, and he added thoughtfully, "Tell Amos to go with him. They'll be gone a few weeks, and Lee and Brian should be gone by the time they get back."

Brock was the middleman for Ike when it came to trading rifles to the Indians. Ike was partners with two brothers named Morgan and Boyle Gant, and they were supposed to meet at Bronc, New Mexico, and exchange rifles for pelts every eight weeks.

Butch nodded thoughtfully and said, "I'll tell them soon as we get back to the ranch."

Ike nodded, satisfied, and it was silent as they trotted on.

105

Chapter thirty-one

I spotted Jeremiah behind the bar as we went downstairs. He spotted us at the same time, and he looked uncomfortable.

Ross stood by the stairs, and he shot me a warning look as I walked by.

But I ignored him. I stopped beside the bar when I was even with Jeremiah, but I kept my eyes pointed forward.

"April keeps her job," I said in a quiet and stern voice.

"I never thought otherwise," Jeremiah insisted.

"If you mistreat her," I warned. "I'll kill you."

"I have no intentions of mistreating her," he sounded surprised. "I'm not like that."

"Don't forget it," I said, and then I walked towards the door.

"Lee," Jeremiah called out. "I'm sorry how this all turned out."

I paused at the door and looked back at him.

"No you're not," I said.

***

We went to the livery stable, saddled our horses, and stuffed our belongings into our saddlebags. We led our horses out into the street, and I spotted Jessica Tussle walking up the sidewalk.

"I'll be right back," I told Brian.

I looped my reins around the hitching post and walked towards her. Jessica spotted me, and her body stiffened.

"Jessica," I offered a difficult smile of apology as I stopped in front of her. "I'd like to explain."

She lifted her chin and crossed her arms.

"All right."

I took in a big breath and launched into the story. Afterwards, I watched her face closely for signs of understanding.

There were none. Instead, she gave me a cold, contemptuous look.

"I *trusted* you with all that money."

"Yes, ma'am, you did."

"And you threw it away in one poker game."

"That wasn't my intention."

"That money was all I had," she muttered. "Didn't you know that?"

"I feel terrible, Jessica. I really do."

"Yancy told me once that you were no good, but I ignored him," Jessica declared, and I got the feeling that she was talking more to herself than to me. "I should have listened. Yancy may not be much of a talker, but at least he's honest and straightforward."

I felt my neck getting hot.

"Yes, ma'am."

Jessica turned dark, cold eyes on me and said evenly, "Lee Mattingly, long as I live, I never want to see you again."

Her words stung. I couldn't speak, so I hung my head and nodded.

Without another word, she turned and walked away briskly. I watched her until she had disappeared into a hotel down the street, and she never looked back.

Chapter thirty-two

Brian and I rode north in stunned silence. We had things to say, but first we needed time to think on what had just happened.

There was a creek about a mile from town, and we turned and followed it. We found a nice sheltered spot, and we dismounted, picketed our horses, and made camp.

Brian built a fire while I filled our coffee pot with water from the creek, and then we sat around the fire and watched the coffee boil. Soon as it was ready we filled our cups and leaned back.

We still didn't talk. Instead, we just sat there and drank coffee with brooding faces.

Brian finally looked at me and cleared his throat.

"Well, I sure didn't see that coming."

I nodded in agreement.

"Are you all right?" Brian studied me.

"I'm just enjoying my usual twilight sadness, is all."

Brian smiled faintly. He took a swig of coffee and wiped his mouth with his sleeve.

"Well, do you remember what Jessica looks like now?"

The image of her glare flashed in my memory.

"Yes. I don't think I'll be forgetting anytime soon neither."

"She sure was mad."

"She had a right to be. We lost her hotel."

Brian nodded slowly.

"Everything happened so fast," he said wistfully.

"It did," I nodded.

"Almost like it was planned."

"I think it was," I replied slowly.

"How's that?"

"Ike, Jeremiah, Amos; they were all in it together," I declared.

"How do you know?"

"I just do," I grumbled.

"What about April?"

For some reason, the mere mention of her name gave me an odd homesick feeling in the pit of my stomach.

"What about her?"

"Do you think she was in on it too?"

"Of course not," I glared at him. "What gave you that idea?"

"You said they were all in on it."

"Well not her," I frowned. "Everybody else *but* her. Mebbe Ross too, although he sure didn't help us any."

"What could he do? Everything was legal."

I grunted in response.

"Too bad about Jeremiah," Brian said. "He didn't seem like all that bad a feller. I sorta liked him."

"He cheated us," I retorted.

"Mebbe so, but at least he was nice about it."

I grunted again and shook my head.

"Are we going to drift on like Ike suggested?" Brian changed the subject.

"Only a guilty man runs," I replied stubbornly, and added, "We've done nothing wrong."

"But Ike said-."

"I don't care what Ike said," I interrupted.

"So what are we going to do?"

I listened to the question, and it was silent as I pondered it. I turned it around in my head, studied it from all angles, and decided.

"We're going to get our hotel back," I announced.

Brian looked up, surprised.

"How?"

"Easy," I laughed, but not humorously. "We'll just shoot everybody that deserves it."

"That won't get our hotel back," Brian pointed out.

"Mebbe not, but it'll sure make me feel better."

109

Brian looked thoughtful as he took another swig of coffee. Meanwhile, I refilled my cup and leaned back. Several minutes passed, and I looked at Brian and grinned wolfishly.

"Well, it can't possibly get any worse," I said. "We have nothing else to lose."

"We're still alive, ain't we?" Brian disagreed.

"For now," I agreed.

Chapter thirty-three

Brock didn't like having to stay at the ranch, and he was anxious to do something.

Ike and the others rode in midafternoon, and Butch told him and Amos about going to Bronc.

Brock was pleased. He talked it over with Amos, and they agreed to leave now. They packed two mules with the rifles, saddled their horses, and packed a few belongings.

It was late afternoon when they rode out, and Brock figured they could travel at least four or five miles before they had to make camp.

Brock led one of the mules, and Amos led the other one. They found a cow trail that went north, and they followed it in a slow trot.

The country was open, with small rolling hills. They made good time, even with the mules.

Brock's mule started limping about an hour before dark. They went a bit further, but then he started limping even worse.

They dismounted, and already Brock could see the swelling in the back ankle. He cursed softly as he thought the situation over.

"That mule isn't making this trip," Amos commented as he peered down at the ankle.

Brock nodded sourly.

"Are we going back to the ranch?" Amos asked.

"No, we'd lose too much time."

"So what are we going to do?"

Brock gestured to some cliffs that were to the west.

"There's a run down little ranch on the other side of those cliffs. It's run by a bunch of Mexicans. They should have a mule."

"Do you think they'll trade for a crippled mule?" Amos looked doubtful.

Brock didn't answer. Instead, he just grinned wolfishly.

Chapter thirty-four

We woke with the bright sun shining in our faces. It was late, long after sunup, but we didn't mind. We were in no hurry to go anywhere.

We rolled up our bedrolls, and then we stirred the coals, boiled some coffee, and sat around the fire.

Even after a night's sleep I still felt drained and discouraged, and I could tell that Brian felt the same way.

We just sat there until late morning.

I had just built the fire back up when we heard a noise. It was the sound of a horse, and it was coming closer.

I glanced at Brian. Without a word, he grabbed his rifle while I drew my Colt. We backed into some bushes and waited.

"Hello the camp!" A yell sounded out.

"Who's out there?" I replied.

"Ross Stewart. Can I come in?"

I frowned distastefully. I wanted to say no, but instead I yelled, "Come on in if you want."

Brian and I returned to the fire, and we watched quietly as Ross rode in.

He looked timid and nervous. He flashed us a shaky grin, but neither Brian nor I returned it.

"What are you doing here?" I asked in a gruff voice.

"Looking for you," Ross replied. "I figured you would camp by the creek, so I've been following it."

"Why find us?" I asked.

Ross didn't reply. Instead, he sat on his horse and studied us.

"You're both upset," he finally commented.

"Is it obvious?"

"I don't blame you," Ross said. "And I feel bad. I really do. But you know how Ike is. Everything appeared legal. My hands were tied."

"You rode all the way out here just to say that?" I scowled.

"Partly," he replied. "I've also got some news."

"Let's hear it."

"Do you know Miguel Ortiz?"

I thought for a moment.

"Sure. He lives to the north."

"He rode into town this morning all upset. He says two men stole one of his mules last night."

"Why does this concern us?"

"Miguel said that it was two big men, and one of them had red hair. They rode up to the corrals with a lame mule. One of them covered the house with his rifle while the other one switched out the mules. They left the crippled mule in the corral."

I frowned thoughtfully.

"You think it was Brock and Amos?"

"The description fits."

"Are you going after them?"

"No, I've got to stay in town," Ross replied. "But, I thought you two might be interested."

"We are," I said, and I glanced at Brian. He nodded, so I looked back at Ross. "We'll go take a look."

"That'll be fine."

It fell silent then, and Ross looked uncomfortable.

"I'd better get back to town," he finally said.

We nodded, but didn't say anything.

"I'm sorry about what happened," Ross tried again. "If I could have done something, I would have. I hope you know that."

We nodded again, and Ross frowned and kicked up his horse.

We didn't say anything as we watched him ride out.

114

Chapter thirty-five

We packed up camp, saddled our horses, and headed north. It was only a few miles to Miguel's ranch, and we arrived early afternoon.

The ranch headquarters was old and run down. We met Miguel at the barn, and he was still upset and excited. We had to listen as he told us the story again, and he led us to the corrals and showed us the tracks.

I dismounted and studied the ground. After a moment I was able to confirm that there had been two of them, and the tracks left out going northwest.

"Do you think it's them?" Brian asked me.

"Only one way to find out," I replied. I stepped back into the saddle and looked at Miguel. "We'll find your mule, amigo."

He thanked us, and we left out. The tracks were easy to follow, and we trotted in a brisk trot.

We went a few miles, and then we rode up to where they had camped. We looked around a bit and pushed on.

"Those mules are slowing them down some," I said as I studied the tracks. "We should catch them tonight."

"What will we do then?" Brian wanted to know.

"We'll get some answers."

Brian frowned thoughtfully and nodded in response.

***

By late afternoon the tracks started getting fresh, and they turned to the north a bit. There was a steep cliff up ahead, and we slowed our pace as we climbed it.

We could see a long ways from the top of the cliff, so we pulled up and studied the landscape.

115

The country in front of us flattened out. There were a few trees scattered about, but other than that there wasn't much cover.

I turned in the saddle, dug in my saddlebags, and pulled out my eyeglass. I took my time as I studied the skyline.

Suddenly, I sat up straight in the saddle.

"I see them," I said softly as I squinted through the eyeglass. "I can't tell for sure, but it looks like they're making camp."

"Can you tell if its Brock and Amos?"

"No, they're too far out."

"So what's the plan?"

I pinched my face in thought.

"It'd be to our advantage if we could surprise them."

"Probably so," Brian agreed.

"It's too open down there," I reasoned, and then I glanced at the sun. "It'll be dark soon, so we'll wait and ride up closer. Then we'll walk up on foot."

Brian nodded, and it fell silent.

We dismounted and sat in some shade. I smoked a cigar to pass the time, and for some reason I kept thinking about April. That made me irritable, and by dark I was restless and ready to move.

We climbed into the saddle and nudged our horses forward. We went about a mile, and we spotted the glow of a campfire in the distance.

"There they are," I pointed.

Brian nodded, and we rode on.

We finally came to some trees that were scattered around an old lakebed. We dismounted and tied our horses in amongst the trees, and then we checked our weapons. We both had Colts, but Brian also carried his Henry rifle.

"You ready?" I asked softly.

Brian nodded, so we walked towards the camp.

"When the shooting starts, I'll take Brock and you take Amos," I said.

116

"You watch Brock," Brian warned. "He's really good with that Colt of his."

"I'm good too," I reminded, "but you're just used to me."

Chapter thirty-six

I could smell something cooking as we got closer, and I could also smell some coffee.

My gun hand hovered naturally over my Colt handle, and Brian carried his rifle in the crook of his arm. I heard a soft click as he pulled the hammer back.

I felt a coldness coming over me. I thought of the hotel we'd lost, and for some reason April and June's face flashed before me. I was suddenly irritable, but I also felt a hard, lonely feeling in the pit of my stomach.

They heard us coming. They stood and backed into the darkness, and as they did I recognized Brock and Amos.

"It's them," I said softly, and Brian nodded.

"Who's out there?" I heard Brock's voice.

"Lee Mattingly and Brian Clark," I replied curtly. "We're coming in."

I heard a low, amused chuckle.

"Come on in!"

They returned to the fire, and we walked up and stopped about thirty feet from them. Brock stood in front of me, and it was silent as everybody studied each other.

I took a quick look around their camp. They had two mules picketed beside their horses, and I also spotted four crates stacked on the ground.

I looked back at Brock, and a wolfish smile had appeared on his face.

"I'm not in the mood to wave at the angels tonight," he said, and his voice was thick with sarcasm.

"I don't mind that one bit," I replied.

Brock snorted, and asked, "How'd you find us?"

"Miguel. He wants his mule back."

Brock laughed at that, and I glanced at Amos.

His face was tight and drawn. There was also a prideful look in his expression, like he was itching to boast.

I decided to give him a chance.

"I take it you work for Ike," I said in a flat voice.

"That's right. I have been from the start," he scoffed.

"And it was you two that robbed us," I encouraged.

"That was the plan," Amos said, and then he laughed.

"Who broke into the safe?" I prodded for more information.

"I did," Amos boasted. "That's why Ike hired me. There isn't a safe invented that I can't crack."

"And it was also you that attacked me," I said.

Amos nodded, and added, "I enjoyed that too."

"I bet you did," I forced a smile.

"Why are you here, Lee?" Brock spoke back up and changed the subject.

"I told you; Miguel wants his mule back. You boys stole him, so I'm taking you two back to town. You also just confessed to robbing our hotel."

"And if we don't go back?"

I smiled in response.

Brock grunted. He glanced at Amos and looked back at me.

"You're good, but you ain't as good as me," he said.

"What's in the crates?" I asked as I ignored his comment.

"Wouldn't you like to know," Brock sneered.

"As a matter of fact, I would."

"There's only one way you're going to find that out."

"All right then," I nodded.

Brock was enjoying himself, and he took his time. I watched him closely as he faced up to me, and his eyes were hard.

"I've never liked you," he said.

"Funny, I've never liked *you*."

"Let's see who's the best," Brock said, and he grabbed for his Colt.

119

I jumped forward. My arm flexed, and my Colt was in my hand. I aimed effortlessly and pulled the trigger. Flame and smoke exploded from the barrel, and I heard a thumping sound as my bullet hit flesh.

Brock had fired too, but my slight movement forward threw his aim off. I felt the sharp whip of a bullet as it fanned air close to my head, and then I saw Brock stagger backwards. He fell on his back, kicked out, and was still.

Meanwhile, the roar of gunfire was all around me. I glanced sideways, and Brian stood there with his rifle in his hands. He had a wild look on his face, and his arm bled from a slug that had creased him.

Amos lay on the ground, choking and gasping for air.

"You all right?" I asked Brian.

He nodded.

"He nicked me, that's all."

I nodded, relieved, and we both reloaded our weapons. Then, we checked on the downed men.

Brock was dead. However, Amos was still alive, but not for long. Blood was choking him, and it ran out his mouth and down his cheek.

Brian and I squatted on our heels beside him.

"Help me, please," Amos managed.

"Not much we can do," I said as I studied the wounds. "You've got a bullet in your gut and another one in your chest."

"I'm dying," Amos whispered, and his eyes were wide with fright.

"Looks like it," I agreed. It was silent, and I added, "You might as well answer a few questions. Where were you and Brock headed?"

Amos stared at me. A few seconds passed, and then his face relaxed.

"Bronc," he said in a gasping whisper. "There's rifles in the crates. We're supposed to meet the Gant brothers."

"Morgan and Boyle Gant?"

"Yes. They're Ike's partners."

"And they're trading rifles to the Injuns," I figured, and Amos nodded.

I glanced thoughtfully at Brian and looked back at Amos. I started to ask another question, but then I stopped. His eyes had glazed over, and he was dead.

"Well," I said as I stood. "That's that."

Chapter thirty-seven

Brian's arm bled a little, but not bad. I had some bandages in my saddlebags, and I wrapped his arm good and tight.

After that we picketed our horses next to theirs, dug our cups out of our saddlebags, and walked over to the fire.

They had cooked some fried salt pork and biscuits. The biscuits were burned black, but the pork was still edible. We tossed the biscuits into the bushes, poured us some coffee, and sat round the fire and chewed on the pork.

We didn't feel like talking much, so we ate in silence.

I always felt exhausted after a gunfight, and I also got a sick feeling in the pit of my stomach. I glanced at Brian, and I could tell that he felt the same way.

"Well, we got the fellers that robbed us," Brian finally said.

"We did," I nodded.

"But this won't get our hotel back."

"No, it won't," I agreed.

"I wonder what happened to our money?"

"Ike probably has it."

Brian nodded and looked around camp.

"What are we going to do now?" He asked.

"I've been pondering that," I said. "You heard what Amos said. They were on their way to Bronc to meet Morgan and Boyle."

"I heard that, yes."

"I know Morgan. He's a smart, educated feller, but he's no good. He almost killed me once."

"I've heard of them, but I've never met 'em."

"They'll have a long wait before they figure out that Brock and Amos aren't coming," I said, and I smiled at the thought.

"They probably will."

"It would be a shame to keep them waiting," I commented.

Brian looked at me over the rim of his coffee cup.

"What are you getting at?"

"Ike stole our business," I said, and suggested, "Why don't we steal his?"

Brian pinched his face in thought.

"That won't get our hotel back either," he pointed out.

"True," I agreed, and then I started to add, "But, it'll-."

"Make you feel better," Brian interrupted.

"That's right."

Brian gestured at Amos and Brock.

"You said killing them would make you feel better too. Did it?"

"Not yet," I admitted.

"It's a long ride to Bronc," Brian objected.

"It is," I agreed.

It was silent then. A few minutes passed, and we both drank several cups of coffee.

Finally, Brian sighed.

"You're going to Bronc with or without me, aren't you?"

"I reckon so."

"And there's no way I can talk you out of it?"

"Probably not."

Brian studied me a moment and sighed.

"Fine," he muttered. "I'll ride along then."

I smiled and nodded.

"What about April?" Brian asked suddenly, and the mention of her name made me jump.

"What about her?"

"Should we ride back to town and tell her we'll be gone for a while? You told her we'd be around."

I was startled by the question, and I frowned irritably to cover my surprise.

"Why would I do that?"

"I thought you, her, and June were getting along pretty good."

"We were friends."

"It seemed like more than that to me."

"That's all it was," I said sharply, and asked, "What gave you that idea?"

"Only what I saw."

I snorted, and it was silent while I searched for the right words.

"She's had it rough this past year. But, she's also a nice lady, and June's a good kid too," I said. "As much as they've been through, I figured they needed a friend. That's all."

"If you say so."

"I say so," I said firmly.

Brian nodded and took a swig of coffee.

Chapter thirty-eight

We were up early. We cooked some breakfast, and afterwards we unpacked our shovels and buried Brock and Amos.

After that we turned our attention to the livestock.

We messed around with their horses, and we discovered that they were both extremely gentle. So, we decided to use them instead of the mules to pack the rifles. We packed them down, and they didn't give us any trouble.

We turned the mules loose. We figured Miguel's mule would drift back home, and the other mule would probably go with him. We reckoned Miguel could have the extra mule for his troubles, plus the crippled mule.

There was nothing else to tend to, so we packed up camp, climbed on our horses, and took out going north.

***

It took us eight days to reach Bronc. We traveled mostly in a slow trot, and we made good time.

The loss of our hotel still stung, and we didn't talk much about it. I figured the pain would ease as time went along, but it didn't. Instead, anger slowly built inside me, and I was more determined than ever to bring Ike down.

I also missed my morning breakfasts with June and my conversations with April. I tried hard not to think about them, but their faces refused to leave my memory.

We camped that final night about a mile from Bronc. We unsaddled and picketed the horses, cooked up some supper, and afterwards we sat around the fire and made plans.

"Morgan would probably recognize me," I said, and Brian nodded.

"I think it would be best if we pulled them away from town," I suggested. "Be less witnesses that way."

"What do you have in mind?"

"You could ride into town and meet them, and then bring them back here."

"Then what?"

I smiled, but didn't reply.

Brian studied me thoughtfully and nodded.

"All right," he said. "I'll ride into town in the morning."

I nodded and took a swig of coffee.

Chapter thirty-nine

Brian Clark woke at sunup. After breakfast he saddled his horse, said goodbye to Lee, and took off towards town.

He traveled in a slow trot. It was a clear morning, and the warm sun felt good on his back.

He was still hesitant about going up against the Gant brothers. If it had been up to him, they would have forgotten about Ike and drifted on.

But Lee was twenty years younger and more impulsive. Lee was also his friend, and Brian had always been loyal to his friends. So he would stay with Lee until the bitter end, whatever that might be.

Brian had never been to Bronc, and he was surprised at how small it was. There were only three buildings. There was a livery stable, a trading post, and a cantina.

He felt uncomfortable as he rode in. The street was dry and dusty, and little whirlwinds swirled around him.

The street was empty, except for two horses that were tied to the hitching rail in front of the cantina.

The horses looked familiar, and Brian frowned as he tried to place where he had seen them. But he couldn't remember, so he dismounted and tied his horse to the hitching rail.

He stepped up onto the front porch. He reached down and felt his Colt, and it gave him a reassuring feeling. He breathed deeply and walked through the swinging doors.

He paused inside the doorway. He let his eyes adjust, and then he glanced around.

The cantina wasn't much of a place. It was dark, and it smelled of whiskey, sweat, and cigar smoke. There were a few tables spread about, and the bar was two long planks laid on top of two whiskey kegs.

A fat Mexican stood behind the bar. He looked unconcerned and uninterested.

127

Two men were seated at a table in the back corner. There was a dark shadow that fell across their table, and he couldn't see their faces very well. However, he could tell that one was big and wide shouldered, and the other one was small and hard bodied.

There was a coffee pot on the table, and they both held cups. The cup partly hid the smaller one's face as Brian walked towards them.

Brian finally got a good look at their faces, and he stopped midstride. His mouth fell open, and he was visually shaken.

The men at the table were studying Brian, and they frowned curiously when they recognized him.

"Well now," Cooper Landon said calmly. "If it isn't Brian Clark."

"Sure is," Yancy Landon agreed, and he frowned curiously at Brian. "What are you doing here?"

Chapter forty

To wait can be the hardest part, especially when you're expecting trouble.

But morning came and went, and Brian didn't return. I was confused, because I was close enough to town to hear any gunfire, but so far there hadn't been any.

Still, I knew something had gone wrong. I saddled my horse, checked my Colt, stepped into the saddle, and trotted towards town.

I had an odd feeling in the pit of my stomach, and I felt a coldness coming over me like I'd never felt before. I don't know how, but I sensed that a danger like no other was waiting for me.

I pulled up at the outskirts of town. I studied the lone street, and I spotted Brian's horse tied beside two others at the cantina. Other than that, the street was empty.

The livery stable was the nearest building. I rode over to it, dismounted, and tied my horse to the hitching rail. Then, I walked slowly towards the cantina.

My face was hard as flint, and my heart thumped wildly. My mouth was dry, and my legs trembled in anticipation.

I was halfway to the cantina when I heard the livery stable door open behind me. It made a slow, eerie sounding creak.

"Lee Mattingly," a cold, stern voice said.

I stopped in the street. I turned around slowly, and my gun-hand hovered naturally over my gun handle.

Yancy Landon stood in front of me. His face was emotionless, and he looked ready to draw. I also noticed a Texas Ranger badge pinned on his vest.

The wind was blowing some, and little dirt devils swirled around us.

I was surprised to see him, but I managed to hide it. A few seconds passed as I thought on it, and I smiled and chuckled as I came to a decision.

"Hello, Yancy," I drawled.

"Lee."

"You're a Texas Ranger now?"

"I am."

"How did that happen?"

"It happened," Yancy said, and declared, "You're under arrest."

"I don't think I want to be arrested today."

"I don't care what you want."

"Where's Cooper?" I asked.

"He's around."

"How about Brian?"

"He's with Coop."

I nodded, and with my left hand I reached up and scratched my jaw.

"What are you doing here, Yancy?"

"I could ask you the same thing."

I nodded and smiled sadly.

"I messed things up."

"I can see that."

"Have you seen Jessica?" I asked.

"Yes."

"How is she?"

"Fine."

I chuckled.

"You've never been one to talk much."

Yancy ignored my remark.

"I'm taking you in, Lee."

"No," I shook my head. "You're not."

"I don't want to kill you."

"I know," I said softly, and added, "I think we've both known that someday, it would come to this."

"Unbuckle your gun belt," Yancy tried again.

"Can't."

"Why not?" Yancy looked at me hard.

"There's always been an unanswered question between us," I explained.

"What's that?"

"Who's best."

"That's a bunch of foolishness," Yancy retorted.

"It ain't for me."

Yancy glared at me, and I smiled back. He studied me a moment more and narrowed his eyes.

"You do what you think is best then," he said, and I nodded.

"If you live, tell Jessica I'm sorry," I said.

"Sorry for what?"

"She'll understand."

Yancy nodded, and it fell silent.

My heart thumped as we stared at each other. Several seconds passed, and then we grabbed for our Colts.

My hand hadn't even touched my handle when a thunderous boom bellowed out, and I felt a hard kick hit my shoulder.

The impact twirled me viciously. I hit the ground hard, and a pain shot throughout my body.

I grimaced and shook my head to clear the cobwebs. But it didn't work, and then I heard running footsteps.

My head was swirling, and I was disorientated. I closed my eyes and moaned as I passed out.

Chapter forty-one

I woke up with a soft groan. The first thing I realized was that my shoulder was hurting and throbbing.

I heard somebody arguing, and I recognized Yancy and Cooper Landon's voices.

"Don't you ever – and I mean ever – do that again," Yancy was saying.

"You mean save your life?" Cooper asked calmly.

"It's not my life you saved; it's his."

Cooper's reply was muffled. I groaned again, and I heard footsteps walking towards me.

"He's waking up," Cooper commented.

I forced my eyes open, blinked, and looked at my surroundings.

I was in the livery stable, lying on my back next to a stall. Yancy Landon stood next to the gate, and he was watching me with an emotionless face. Meanwhile, Cooper squatted on his heels beside me.

"How you feeling?" He asked.

I didn't answer. Instead, I continued to look around, and I spotted a boy standing in the corner. He was around twelve or so, and he was watching me with a somber face.

I stared at him for several seconds, and then I looked at Cooper. He was waiting for a reply, so I swallowed and licked my lips.

"I feel like I've been shot," I managed.

"That's cause you were," Cooper said. "Josie's already looked at your shoulder. She says it's not too bad."

"Josie's here?"

Cooper nodded.

"She's out looking for a stick," he said.

"What for?" I narrowed my eyes.

"You'll find out soon enough," Cooper grinned.

132

I was confused by that remark, but I was too tired to try and figure it out.

"Where's Brian?" I asked instead.

"He rode out to pack up your camp. He should be back soon."

"You let him go off by himself?"

"We trust him."

I grunted, and then I winced as my shoulder throbbed with pain.

A few seconds passed, and then I nodded at the boy.

"Who's that?"

"This is Wyatt," Cooper smiled at him. "Me and Josie have adopted him. Ain't that right, Wyatt?"

The boy nodded, but that was all.

"He doesn't talk much," Cooper informed me.

"So he and Yancy have something in common," I smiled weakly.

Cooper smiled back, and I breathed deeply and looked at Yancy.

"Well, you got me," I said quietly.

"That is correct."

"I always thought I was faster than you, but I didn't even touch my gun handle," I muttered.

"Neither did I," Yancy said.

I frowned at that.

"What?"

"It wasn't me that shot you," Yancy informed.

"Oh? Then who did?" I asked, confused.

"Cooper. He shot you from the cantina window with his rifle."

I looked at Cooper, and he nodded.

"Why'd you do that for?" I scowled.

"I'd like to know that too," Yancy added as he shot his brother a dark look.

Cooper smiled as he stood from his crouch.

"Someday, I just might tell you," his eyes twinkled.

"Tell me what?" I demanded.

Cooper didn't reply, and Yancy and I scowled at him.

***

Brian Clark rode back in, and he looked relieved to find me awake.

"Are you all right?" He asked.

"Not really," I replied.

He smiled faintly and started unsaddling our horses.

He was almost done when Josie walked in, and she carried a long stick.

Josie was small and slim. She also had a sharp, young-looking face with long, brown hair.

She and I had some history together. A while back the Oltman brothers captured her from the Indians, and I ended up with her soon after that. I sort of looked after her, and for a while I was very fond of her. But then she chose Cooper, and that was that.

"Josie," I nodded at her. "How are you?"

"Good."

"I'm glad to hear that."

Josie gestured at my shoulder.

"I fix."

"That'll be fine," I smiled and nodded.

Chapter forty-two

Josie patched me up, and it was one of the most painful experiences I have ever gone through.

She built a fire in the back, and she whittled down one end of the stick. She placed the whittled end in the fire, and then Cooper and Brian got ahold of me.

Yancy didn't help any. Instead, he and Wyatt just stood there and watched. Yancy had an interested look on his face, like he knew what was coming.

Using Cooper's knife, Josie dug the bullet out of my shoulder, and that was painful enough. But then, without warning, she pulled the stick out of the fire, and it was bright red and glowing. She firmly pressed the burning end into my wound, and it made a hissing sound as the heat seared my flesh. It hurt something awful, and Cooper and Brian had to keep a firm grip on me.

After that she packed my wound with mud, and the wetness cooled the burning sensation some. After the mud dried, she cleaned my shoulder and bandaged it.

I was surprised to find that it wasn't bleeding anymore. But it was mighty painful, and already my shoulder was sore and stiff.

"Feel better?" Cooper asked me.

I grunted in response, and Cooper grinned.

"You'll heal quick enough, but you'll have a nasty scar. I know from experience."

"I think it would have been better if Brian had just stitched it up," I grumbled.

"Possible, but it'll heal faster this way."

"I didn't know I was in such a hurry."

"You might be," Cooper said.

"And why is that?"

Yancy cleared his throat, and I looked at him.

135

"While you were unconscious, Brian told us why you came here. He also told us about losing the hotel, and about Brock and Amos."

I frowned at Brian, but his face remained blank.

"All right; you know why we're here," I said as I looked back at Yancy. "What are you doing here?"

"We killed the Gant brothers a while back," Yancy announced, and I was startled. "We came here, posing as the Gant brothers, to capture Brock."

"We were hoping to talk to him," Cooper added. "We had a deal to offer."

"What sort of deal?" I asked curiously.

"Ike has several men working for him, all over Texas," Cooper informed. "He also has a man inside Huntsville prison. Every time one of Ike's men gets sent there, they escape."

"In exchange for a full pardon, we were hoping to send Brock to Huntsville to find out who Ike's inside man is," Yancy added.

"Brock would have never agreed to that," I said as I thought on it. "He was too loyal to Ike."

"It doesn't matter now," Yancy said sourly.

An idea suddenly occurred to me, and I pinched my face in thought.

"How 'bout sending me to Huntsville?" I suggested. "I could take Brock's place."

Yancy was startled, and he narrowed his eyes as he studied me.

"Why would you want to do that?"

"Ike Nash humiliated me," I explained bitterly. "I'll do whatever it takes to take him down."

Yancy glanced at Cooper, and he scratched his jaw as he thought on that.

"I could go with you," Brian spoke up. "You could be Brock, and I'll be Amos."

"Are you sure?" I frowned at him.

136

Brian nodded, and I was humbled by his loyalty. I nodded back, and then we looked at Yancy.

"All right," Yancy finally said. "I'll offer you two the same deal. Find out who Ike's man is, and you'll both receive a full pardon."

I nodded and asked, "When do we get started?"

"We'll stay here until you can ride, and then we'll send you to Hunstville," Yancy replied.

"I'm sure you'll enjoy that," I said sourly.

"I think I will," Yancy replied, and he smiled a rare smile.

Chapter forty-three

We left Bronc eight days later.

My shoulder was still sore and stiff. But, it had healed for the most part, and I could ride.

We rode south to El Paso, and Yancy turned us over to a company of Texas Rangers.

We couldn't risk telling them who we were, so we were treated like actual prisoners once we reached El Paso. They shackled our hands and feet, and it was a somber feeling.

Yancy and Cooper left us there, and they headed back to Midway. They took our horses and gear, and Cooper said he'd look after our belongings while we were in prison.

We were transported to Huntsville in a prisoner wagon. The Texas Rangers called it a 'tumbleweed wagon' because the wagon wandered along aimlessly.

We picked up three other prisoners on our way. Two were convicted murderers, and the other one was a bank robber. We were all chained to the floor of the wagon, and at nighttime we were chained to the trees. If no trees were available, we were chained to the wagon wheels.

It took us several weeks to get there, and when we arrived we were sweaty, dirty, and in need of a bath.

The bouncing in that wagon didn't help my shoulder any. But, complaining wouldn't have done any good, so I kept my mouth shut.

Unpleasant as our trip was, the severity of our decision didn't hit home until they slammed the gate shut at Huntsville prison.

They unloaded us, stuck us in a stonewalled room, stripped us, gave us crude haircuts, and threw buckets of cold water on us. After that they gave us a pair of striped prison clothes. We got dressed, and they made us stand in a line.

The captain of the guards came in to see us next.

He had a leathery face with a hard jaw and cold eyes. Even if he had wanted to look friendly, I doubted that he could with that face.

He wasn't trying to look friendly now. He thrust his jaw out as he paced back and forth in front of us, and his voice had a hard ring of authority.

"My name's Reilly Parker," he bellowed. "From here on out, you boys belong to me. You stay on my good side and life can be pleasant. But you make me mad-," his voice got even harder, "-then I'll make your sorry lives so miserable you'll wish you were dead. Do you understand me?"

"Yes, sir!" We all said.

"Everyone earns their keep here, and you five will be no different. You'll work six days a week. If you behave, you'll have Sundays off." He paused and looked at us. "Everything goes through me. If any of you boys want to write a letter to your mama, just ask and you'll be given pen and paper. *If* I approve of the letter, I'll send it on." He paused again and looked at the guards. "That's all for now. Take them to their cells."

A guard shoved me in the back. I stumbled forward, but managed to stay on my feet. Then, I hurried after the others.

We marched outside, and the sun was bright. I squinted as I looked around, and we were in the prison yard.

Other inmates stared at us while we marched across the yard. I heard a few chuckles, but I ignored them as we went back inside where the cells were.

I studied the cells as we walked down the long hallway. They were roughly eight by eight, and the walls were made out of red adobe bricks.

The guards stopped at a cell, and one of them unlocked the iron door and gestured at Brian and me. We walked in, and he slammed the door shut behind us. The sound was loud, and Brian and I both jumped.

139

We stood by the door and watched as they walked on down the hallway.

Soon as they were gone, we looked at each other. Brian's face was somber and grave, and I'm sure mine looked the same way.

I turned and studied our cell.

There were four bunks; two on either side. There was a bucket in the corner, and it smelled. I figured out right quick that the bucket was our outhouse.

I suddenly noticed that we had company.

Lying in a bunk was a man. He was reading a book, and it looked like a law book of some sort.

He ignored us, and it was silent as I studied him.

He had brown hair and dark skin, and he was so thin that a stiff wind could have blown him over.

There was also a look about him that told me he was dangerous. I knew right off that he wasn't one to mess with.

"Afternoon," I said.

He took his eyes off the book and looked at us. His eyes were cold and hard. He studied us a moment, and he returned to his book without saying a word.

I glanced at Brian, and he looked concerned. He motioned me closer, and I leaned in so he could whisper in my ear.

"Do you know who that is?" He murmured.

I shook my head.

"That's John Wesley Hardin!" He hissed.

I stared at Brian, and he nodded emphatically. Several seconds passed, and then I smiled.

"I'd be worried, if'n I was you," I whispered back.

"Why's that?"

"He once killed a man just for snoring," I explained.

Brian's eyes grew wide. I chuckled softly, and we walked over and sat on the bunk that was across the cell from Hardin.

140

We just sat there, looking at him, and Hardin continued to ignore us as he read his book.

It started to get dark about an hour later. I suddenly realized how tired I was, so I climbed into the top bunk while Brian stretched out below me.

Hardin finally shut the book and rolled over. A few minutes passed, and we could hear the steady sound of his breathing.

I glanced down at Brian, and he was wide-awake.

"Can't sleep?" I whispered.

Brian gestured at Hardin.

"I want to make sure he's sound asleep first."

"Good luck with that."

"You ain't worried?" Brian hissed.

"I don't snore," I whispered back.

Chapter forty-four

No other prisoners were added to our cell, so it was just Hardin and us.

The guards let all of us prisoners out of our cells at sunup, and we were herded to the mess hall.

It was a big square room, with tables in long rows. Brian and I were at the back of the line, and I studied the other prisoners.

At least half of the inmates were dark, either Mexicans or Indians. The rest were white, except for one Chinaman.

A sour-looking cook filled our plates with scrambled eggs and two biscuits. There wasn't any coffee, just water.

We stood there and studied the sitting arrangement. The Indians sat together, the Mexicans sat together, and the whites sat together. We found an open spot among the whites and sat down.

Nobody talked much during breakfast. Afterwards, we grabbed our plates, and as we left the mess hall we put our spoons, plates, and cups in battered tubs.

Outside in the yard the guards lined us up, and they split us up according to our different duties.

Brian and I were assigned to the brickyard. I wasn't sure what that was, but I figured out right quick that it was where adobe bricks were made.

The Walls Unit was the nickname of the division of the prison that we were in, and the walls were made out of red adobe bricks. We soon discovered that most of the adobe bricks were made at Huntsville.

There was a big mixing trough in the middle of the yard, and next to that were the brick molds. On the other side of the trough were two wagons. One was heaped full with sand, and the other one was heaped full of reddish clay.

"You two are the mixers," one of the guards told us. "Take your shoes off and climb into the trough."

"What are we mixing?" I asked.

"Clay, sand, and water."

"What do we mix with?"

"Your feet. Stomp it until it's a thick mud, and then these other fellers will fill the molds."

I looked at Brian and scowled, but we did as we were told.

Everyone else got in their place.

Two men climbed into the wagons and shoveled clay and sand into the trough while others poured water in. No shovels were allowed, so they had to shovel the sand with their hands. Meanwhile, the rest of the crew stood by the molds and waited.

"All right," the guard commanded us. "Sweat never drowned anybody, so get to it!"

Brian and I started stomping with our feet. We stomped, and stomped, and stomped.

As we stomped, they poured in more water. But then it got too runny, so they shoveled in more clay and sand. But then it got too thick, so the process started all over again. Meanwhile, Brian and I stomped furiously.

We finally got the correct mixture of mud, and one of the guards motioned at us.

"All right, get out of there. Soon as they get the mud into the molds we'll start again."

We climbed out, walked over to the water barrel, and we drank like men who had been lost in the desert for days.

Brian's shirt was soaked with sweat, and he was panting hard. He looked at me and smiled as I gulped down more water.

"What are you smiling about?" I frowned as I wiped the sweat from my brow.

"I was just wondering," he replied.

"Wondering what?"

"Wondering if we're finally getting what we deserve," he explained.

143

That was a depressing thought, and my face got heavy and mulish.

"Probably," I admitted.

Chapter forty-five

It didn't take me long to decide that I never wanted to see a brick, let alone make one, for the rest of my life.

We worked until late afternoon, and the guards finally decided that we'd made enough bricks for one day. We washed up and made our way to the mess hall.

I felt a weariness like I'd never felt before. I had worn blisters on my feet, and my legs were heavy. They hurt so bad that they even trembled as I stood in line for supper.

After supper the prisoners were allowed to stroll around the prison yard, but Brian and I went straight to our cell. Hardin was there, reading his book, but we ignored him.

I was hurting so bad that Brian had to help me climb into my bunk, and then he wearily fell into his.

A few minutes passed, and we both moaned and groaned.

"I'm too old for this," Brian muttered.

"So am I," I said.

"You're twenty years younger than I am," he retorted.

"True, but I'm catching up mighty quick."

"What's the plan?" Brian asked, and he must have forgotten that Hardin was there. "I don't think I can take too much more of this."

"What plan?" I said, and I glanced down at him and made a motion to be quiet.

Brian's eyes grew wide, and it was silent for several tense seconds.

We heard a chuckle. We looked at Hardin, and he closed his book, sat up in his bunk, and looked sourly at us.

"Don't tell me," he said, and I was surprised at how educated he sounded. "You two are already planning an escape."

"Who said anything about an escape?" I asked innocently.

145

"Whatever you have planned, don't try it," he said as he ignored my comment. "I've tried everything, and nothing works."

We didn't say anything, and Hardin continued.

"I've tried tunneling out from the wheelwright's shop, I've made keys to the locks; I've even bribed the guards."

"What went wrong?" Brian asked.

"This prison is filled with Benedict Arnolds," Hardin said bitterly. "You'll find that out soon enough."

"What happened when you were caught?" I asked curiously.

"They tied my hands and feet, stretched me out, and flogged me with a strap until I was quivering and bleeding," Hardin said, and his face was twisted in pain as he remembered back.

"Are you going to attempt another escape?" Brian asked.

Hardin laughed, but not humorously. He leaned back in his bunk, opened his book, and went back to ignoring us as he started reading.

Brian looked at me, and I just shrugged.

Chapter forty-six

Life in prison quickly became a routine. We ate breakfast, made adobe bricks, ate supper, strolled around in the prison yard, slept, and then we did it all over again the next day.

I discovered that nighttime in prison was a good time to reflect, and I took advantage of it. I thought of our hotel, Jessica, Amos and Brock; I even thought about Yancy.

But mostly, I thought about April and June. I just couldn't forget those big, blue eyes, and they haunted me every time I tried to sleep. It was a confusing and irritating feeling.

A week passed, and we slowly got accustomed to the strenuous work. Our feet got hard and calloused, and muscles started forming in our legs that I didn't know were even there.

During that week nobody approached us or talked to us much. We both listened, trying to figure out who Ike's man was, but we never heard his name mentioned.

We sat alone at breakfast one morning, talking it over.

"I wonder why Ike's man hasn't contacted us?" Brian wondered.

"Mebbe he doesn't know about us yet."

"Well, somebody had better know *something*," Brian grunted.

"I have a thought," I said, and I stood abruptly.

While Brian watched curiously, I beat on the table with my hand. The chatter in the room died down, and almost everybody in the room looked at me.

"I'd like to propose a toast," I said loudly.

I heard a few mumblings, and everyone stared at me as if I'd lost my mind.

I saw a guard walking towards me, and he held a wood truncheon in his hand.

"Sit down!" He growled.

147

I ignored him as I raised my cup of water.

"To Ike Nash, the greatest man in Texas!"

Nobody said anything. I took a swig of water and sat down as the guard reached us.

"Do that again, and you'll spend a week in solitary confinement," he said harshly.

"Yes, sir."

The guard glared at me for a few seconds more, and then he turned and walked away. Meanwhile, all the prisoners scoffed at me and returned to their breakfast.

"What was that?" Brian hissed.

"I'm just grabbing at every straw that floats by," I whispered back.

"So now what?"

"Now we wait and see."

Chapter forty-seven

At the end of each month, Butch Nelson always made a trip to Empty-lake to buy supplies for the ranch.

After breakfast, he hitched up a team to the buckboard. It was a pleasant day, and he enjoyed the ride to town. He stopped at the general store and went inside.

The general store was a good place to hear the news. There was always a pot of coffee brewing on the stove in the back, and folks liked to gather there and gossip.

Today it was crowded and busy. Butch gave the clerk his list, and his mood darkened as he listened in on the chatter.

The clerk got everything gathered, and Butch paid the bill and loaded the supplies into the back of the backboard. He trotted briskly back to the ranch, tied the team to the hitching rail, and hurried inside.

Ike looked up curiously from his desk as he entered the study.

"Back so soon?"

"There's news from town. Bad news, I'm afraid."

"Oh?"

"It's Yancy and Cooper Landon. They arrested Brock and Amos, and they also killed Morgan and Boyle Gant."

Ike was startled, and an irritated look crossed his face.

"Those Landons are starting to annoy me," he muttered, and asked, "What happened to Brock and Amos?"

"Judge Parker found them guilty."

"Huntsville?"

"Yep."

"That happened fast," Ike grunted.

"What do you want to do?"

It was silent as Ike pondered that.

"I need Brock," he finally said. "Go ahead and make the usual arrangements."

"How 'bout Amos?"

"Might as well."

"I'll get it done," Butch said.

He started to leave the room, but Ike called out and stopped him.

"I received word from Ron Gallegan, and he's coming to see me in a couple of weeks. We'll use the hotel as our meeting place. I want Ron to be treated with the upmost respect."

"I'll make sure Jeremiah understands," Butch said, and then he asked, "Isn't Ron that politician from back east?"

"That's right," Ike nodded. "We've got important business to discuss."

Butch was curious, but he knew not to ask any more questions. He was silent, hoping Ike would explain, but he didn't.

"That's all," Ike told him instead.

Butch nodded curtly and left the study.

Chapter forty-eight

That evening after supper, Brian and I walked around the prison yard. It was cool and pleasant. Prisoners were spread all about, and nobody paid us any attention.

Reilly Parker, the captain of the guards, strolled around the yard with his truncheon in hand. Several of the inmates had written letters, and this was the time that Reilly usually collected them.

Reilly stuffed all the letters into his pocket, and then he walked over to us. He waited while the closest prisoners to us drifted away, and then he lowered his voice.

"I heard you mentioned Ike Nash's name at breakfast," his voice was curt.

I was startled, but I recovered quickly.

"That's right," I nodded. "We work for him."

"Is that so?"

"Sure is," I said, and asked, "Do you know Ike?"

"No, I've never met him," he said. It was quiet, and he added, "But, I've done some work for him from time to time."

I studied his face, but his expression revealed nothing.

"Can you get us out of here?" I finally asked.

He grunted.

"Look. I don't know what you boys think you know, but I haven't heard anything about you two yet. If word comes, I'll let you know. Until then, you boys are nothing to me. So keep your mouth shut and don't be mentioning Ike Nash again."

"Yes, sir," I said.

He scowled at us and moved on, and Brian glanced at me.

"I think we found our man," he said softly.

"Looks like it," I agreed.

"Now what?" Brian asked.

151

"I'm not sure," I frowned.

"Can't we just send word to Yancy?" Brian looked hopeful.

"Sure," I replied sarcastically. "We'll write Yancy a letter, give it to Reilly, and hope he doesn't read it."

"We wouldn't have to mention anything important," Brian objected. "We could just ask Yancy to come visit. Yancy would know."

"That would still raise suspicions," I disagreed. "Two jailbirds writing Yancy Landon? We'd be questioned for sure."

"So what do we do?"

"We'll wait and see what develops."

It was silent as Brian thought on that, and then he sighed.

"I reckon there's not much else we *can* do," he said broodily.

"No, there's not," I agreed.

Chapter forty-nine

Another week came and went.

The only change in our routine was that a new inmate was assigned to the brickyard, and Brian got promoted to shoveling sand. That was an easier job than mixing, and I was glad for Brian.

Reilly Parker came to see us one evening in the prison yard. We were standing in the corner, and we were alone.

"I received word yesterday about you two," he said in a low voice.

"You heard from Ike?" I asked, and there was excitement in my voice.

"Keep your voice down," he growled, and then he nodded. "Ike wants both of you out."

"When?"

"Tonight."

Reilly glanced around. Nobody was watching, so he eased in closer to us. He held something in his hands, and he slipped it to me.

I didn't look, but I could tell that they were keys. With as little movement as possible, I slipped them into my pant's pocket.

"The little key is for the cell, and the bigger one is for the prison yard," Reilly said. "Wait until dark. After things settle down, make your way to the prison yard. There'll be a wagon over by the wheelwright's shop, and you'll find a tarp in the back. Climb in and cover yourselves up. I'll be along directly, and then we'll leave. Got it?"

"I think so," we nodded.

"One last thing," he said. "I'm taking a woman prisoner out of here too. While you two are making your way to the wagon I'll be getting her."

"What if something goes wrong?" Brian spoke up.

"Then you two will be in a lot of trouble," Reilly grunted, and then added, "See you boys tonight."

We nodded, and Reilly strolled away.

Chapter fifty

Life moved at a slow pace in prison, and it seemed even slower after our talk with Reilly Parker.

Prisoners were allowed to stroll around the prison yard until the whistle blew, and we waited impatiently. The whistle finally blew, and all the prisoners made their way to their cells. Once inside, the guards walked down the long hallway and counted us off. Everyone was accounted for, so they slammed the doors shut and left.

Brian paced back and forth at the door. As usual, Hardin ignored us as he read his law book.

"How long should we wait?" Brian hissed at me.

"We'll wait a few minutes and give the guards a chance to get settled," I said.

We heard a chuckle. We turned, and Hardin was looking at us.

"I knew it," he said. "You boys are going to attempt an escape."

"That's right," I confirmed, and then I asked warily, "What are you going to do about that?"

"Nothing," he waved his hand at us. "You won't make it anyway."

"I think we will," I replied.

"What's the plan?"

I reached into my pocket and pulled out the keys, and Hardin snorted.

"I already tried that. You won't get out of the prison yard."

"We'll see."

Hardin snorted again and went back to his book. I studied him a moment, wondering if he was going to cause us trouble, but he seemed absorbed with his reading.

A few minutes passed, and I glanced at Brian.

"You ready?" I asked.

155

He nodded, and I moved to the cell door. I glanced down the hallway, and it was clear as far as I could see.

Being as quiet as possible, I reached through the bars and inserted the key. It made a loud grating sound as I turned the key, and the door opened.

I glanced at Brian and grinned, and we stepped out into the hallway.

As I shut the door I looked back at Hardin, and he was watching us from his bunk.

"I'll see you boys when you get out of solitary confinement," he said.

I didn't have an answer for that, so I just nodded. He nodded back, and we left.

"His confidence in us is overwhelming," Brian whispered wryly.

I smiled, and then we were quiet.

We stayed in the shadows as we went down the hallway, and most of the prisoners didn't even notice us. Those few that did just stared at us.

We reached the door to the prison yard. The yard looked empty, so I rammed the big iron key into the lock and ground it back.

The door opened, and our excitement mounted. We eased into the yard and locked the door behind us.

Keeping low, we crossed a patch of bare ground, cut around the wood shop, and came up behind the wheelwright's shop.

Just as Reilly had said, a team and wagon was in the shadows beside the shop. We hurried over to it, and in the back was a brown tarp. There were also several baskets stacked on the ground beside the wagon.

Moving quickly, we climbed into the back of the wagon and covered ourselves up with the tarp.

I hadn't realized how excited we were. But now, lying under that tarp, we panted hard, and my legs trembled in anticipation.

156

A few minutes passed, but to us it felt like forever.

"What's taking Reilly so long?" Brian sounded irritable.

"He'll be along," I whispered reassuringly.

"What if he doesn't show up?"

That was a disturbing thought, and I frowned.

"I reckon we'll hightail it back to our cell," I said.

"How long do you think we should wait?"

"Let's not get too carried away. He'll be along. Stop worrying."

"It's too late for that."

"Me too," I admitted, and then it fell silent.

Another thirty minutes passed, and we heard some movement.

"Somebody's coming," I whispered, and we hunkered down.

Several tense seconds passed. We heard the sound of footsteps, and they drew close to the wagon and stopped.

"You boys there?" We heard Reilly's voice, and we both breathed a sigh of relief.

"We're here," I said.

"Good. Make room for another passenger."

We scooted over, and Reilly pulled the tarp back. Our heads were down, but I couldn't help but peek at the lady inmate.

She had a small build. She wore dark prison clothes, and she also had a dark shawl that covered her face. Her back was to us as she crawled in beside us.

"Now you three keep quiet," Reilly growled as he covered us back up. "We'll go out the main gate, and I'll have to talk to the guards."

I nodded, but then I realized that he couldn't see me.

"Will do," I said instead.

"Keep quiet!"

I didn't reply. A few seconds passed, and then something heavy was placed on top of us. I was confused,

157

but then I realized that Reilly was putting the baskets that had been beside the wagon on top of us.

We felt a jerk as Reilly climbed onto the wagon seat. He clucked at the horses, and we moved out.

We went a hundred yards or so, and then we stopped. I heard him talking, and I figured we were at the main gate.

I heard footsteps beside the wagon, and I didn't dare breath.

It was then that the woman moved beside me, trying to get comfortable. I winced, but I couldn't do anything.

After what seemed forever, the wagon finally started moving again, and I relaxed a bit. We also picked up speed, and it was real rough under that tarp.

The wagon hit a hard bump in the road, and the lady made a slight whimper. It rocked the wagon, and we rolled back and forth.

We traveled on and on, and the road got rougher. But each second took us further from Huntsville, so I didn't mind.

Another half hour passed, and the lady just couldn't take it anymore.

"I've got to get out," we heard her say. "I'm suffocating under here!"

There was an abrupt movement beside us, and the lady shoved at the baskets and threw the tarp back. We helped, and then we all sat up in the wagon.

My back was to her. I stretched my cramped muscles, and then I turned to greet her.

She turned towards me at the same time, and we were both startled when we saw each other.

It was silent for a few stunned seconds, and her face turned cold and hard.

"It's you," she said in a contemptuous voice.

"Hello, Lucy Wells," I said.

158

Chapter fifty-one

I had forgotten all about Lucy being at Huntsville, but it was obvious that she hadn't forgotten about me. In a mere matter of seconds, her face became twisted with hate.

Lucy was Ike's daughter-in-law, but we had heard that Ike wanted nothing to do with her. He hadn't approved of their marriage, and he was upset when he found out about it.

But Lucy had loved Ike's son Tanner, and she vowed to get revenge when he was killed. But then Judge Parker found her guilty and sent her to Huntsville, and that was the last I'd heard about her.

Brian was stretching his cramped muscles, and he had hadn't seen her yet. Reilly still sat on the wagon seat, and we traveled in a brisk trot.

Lucy and I stared at each other, and her glare turned more hateful with each passing second.

There was a rifle leaning against the seat next to Reilly, and Lucy and I spotted it at the same time.

"Don't," I said tersely, but Lucy ignored me.

We both leaped for the rifle. Our movements spooked the horses, and they lunged into a lope.

"What's going on back there?" Reilly yelled savagely.

We both had our hands on the rifle. She tried desperately to point the barrel in my direction, but I pushed the barrel back.

She suddenly lunged forward as we wrestled for control, and I fell backwards into Brian. We collided hard, and Brian was taken by surprise.

With a loud yell he fell backwards out of the wagon, and I heard a loud thump. He hit the ground rolling and disappeared into the bushes.

Lucy was on top of me, and she had her finger on the trigger as she tried to point the rifle into my gut. But I

159

managed to shove the barrel away right as she pulled the trigger.

The rifle boomed in our hands, and I heard a scream as the bullet hit flesh. We both looked, and Reilly had been hit in the back. The impact threw him forward into the horses, and then he fell.

One of the wheels hit Reilly, and it made a big bump. Lucy was pitched forward, and I fell backwards. The horses were running wild now, and they swerved all over the road.

I had lost my grip on the rifle, and I suddenly realized that Lucy had it. She was leaning against the seat of the wagon, and her eyes were lit up with triumph as she lifted the rifle.

There was no time to defend myself. With a yell, I rolled to my feet and jumped blindly. I heard a rifle shot, and a bullet whistled by my head.

My arms were flailing as I fell. I slammed into the ground, and the impact knocked the breath out of me. I did a few flips and then rolled to a stop.

I gasped for air as I watched the wagon racing away. Lucy had dropped the rifle and had grabbed the reins, and she was trying desperately to slow the horses down.

I got my breath back, and then I sat up and checked myself over. I had scratches and cuts all over, but nothing appeared to be broken.

I stood and looked down the road, and by now the wagon had disappeared into the darkness.

I smiled at that, and then I limped back down the road to find Brian.

Chapter fifty-two

I found Brian knelt beside Reilly Parker.

Even in the moonlight, I could tell that he had scratches all over. There was also a little blood, but other than that he looked fine.

Reilly was lying in the middle of the road, with his mouth open, and his eyes staring at nothing in particular.

"Are you all right?" I asked as I walked up.

"I'll live," Brian said and gestured at Reilly. "But he's dead."

I nodded as I studied him.

"He got shot in the back," I explained.

"What happened in the wagon?"

I explained about Lucy Wells, and Brian looked surprised.

"Of all the women in prison, it had to be her," he grumbled.

"I know."

"I don't think she likes you very much."

"I noticed that," I agreed, and added, "And I'm not the one who killed her husband. Ross did that."

"Do you think she'll come back?"

"No. By the time she gets those horses stopped, she'll be halfway to New Mexico."

Brian nodded thoughtfully while I knelt beside Reilly.

He had a Colt and a gun-belt, and I unbuckled it and looped it around my waist. I checked his pockets next and found sixty dollars.

I stuck the money in my pant's pocket, and we dragged Reilly off the road and covered him up with some brush. Then we stood there and looked around.

There was a full moon, so it wasn't as dark as usual. Near as we could tell, we were in the middle of wide-open hills.

161

We could see the silhouette of some ridges to the west in the far distance, and I gestured at them.

"Let's head for that higher ground," I suggested. "Mebbe we can spot a town or something when it gets daylight."

"We can't just walk into a town," Brian objected as we took out. "We're in prison clothes."

"We'll think of something," I replied.

Chapter fifty-three

I usually didn't care for walking. However, our legs were in good shape on account of stomping bricks, so we didn't mind as much.

We walked all night, and come daylight we reached the top of the ridges. It was a steep climb, and we could see a long ways from the top.

We were afraid of pursuit, and we studied our back trail for movement. To our relief, we didn't see anything.

We turned and studied the country in front of us. There, in the distance, we could see a few buildings scattered about.

"What do you think?" I asked as we squinted our eyes.

"Looks like a village of some sort," Brian commented.

"We need a horse," I said. "Let's go see if they have one we could buy."

"And if they don't?" Brian looked at me.

I didn't answer as I led out.

It was several miles to the buildings, and it took us half the morning to get there.

As we got closer we figured out that it was a small Mexican village.

Small adobe buildings, baked and crumbling in the sun, were scattered all about. Goats, dogs, and children ran all around.

The village was busy and loud, but things quieted down as we walked up, and everybody stared at us.

I'm sure we made a sight. We were hatless, scratched, bruised, and bleeding. On top of that, we were also in prison clothes.

A thin, old Mexican with a white moustache sat by the doorway of the nearest adobe building. A dark, plump woman stood just inside the door, holding a broom. They both watched silently as we walked up.

163

"If nobody makes trouble," I said, "there won't be any. We just want to talk."

They nodded, but that was all.

"This isn't what it looks like," I tried to explain.

The old Mexican remained quiet, and his face was blank.

"All right, mebbe it is what it looks like," I admitted. "But we aren't looking for any trouble. Isn't that right, Brian?"

He nodded.

"We need a horse and a change of clothes," I continued. "We have money."

The old Mexican held up one finger.

"You have a horse?" I asked hopefully.

"Si, but he no look so good," he spoke in broken English.

"Long as I can ride him, I don't care what he looks like," I replied.

"He's gentle, *senor*. Real gentle."

"Let's go have a look," I suggested.

He nodded and stood. He walked with a limp, and everybody watched as we followed after him.

There was a small corral behind the house, and a horse stood by the gate.

I was surprised when I saw him. He was tall, big boned, and mighty stout looking.

"He looks just fine to me," I said, impressed. "How much do you want for him?"

He held up five fingers.

"Five dollars?" I asked, surprised.

"Si," he nodded.

"That's it?" I frowned suspiciously.

He nodded again.

"He no look so good," he repeated.

"We're talking about that horse?" I pointed to the fine, stout looking one in front of us.

164

"Si."

The thought occurred to me that this might be a stolen horse. However, I wasn't about to question our good fortune.

"We'll take him," I said, and asked, "Do you have a saddle we could buy?"

He nodded his head.

"How 'bout some food and clothes?"

"Si," he nodded, and then he headed back towards the house.

I glanced at Brian. He shrugged as we followed after him.

Chapter fifty-four

They fed us a meal of beans and tortillas, and we tore into the food with a vengeance. It was a bland meal, but it tasted wonderful compared to prison food.

After we ate, they fixed us up with some clothes. They were dirty, worn rags, and we could poke our fingers in and out of the holes. But we didn't complain, and it felt good to be wearing something else other than prison clothes.

They also fixed us up with two hats. Brian was given a huge sombrero, and I received a worn out looking hat that looked like a broken tent.

The old Mexican also had plenty of firearms and ammunition. Brian picked out a Colt six-shooter and a rifle, and I got a rifle. We also bought plenty of ammunition.

Next, the old Mexican gave us two brand new pairs of boots. We didn't ask where he got them, and he didn't say. He even threw in two pairs of spurs and two canteens.

I pulled out the sixty dollars from my pocket and gave it all to him. He said it was too much, but I insisted. Then, we went and saddled the horse.

I was still leery about the horse, but he stood perfectly still as I saddled him. I led him around a little, but he wasn't humped up at all.

We stuffed our food and few belongings into the saddlebags, and then I stepped into the saddle. The horse seemed fine, so I offered a hand to Brian and helped pull him up behind me.

"Thank you, amigo," I told the Mexican.

He nodded, and we took out, going west.

***

I was surprised at how well the horse traveled.

166

Big as he was, he had no trouble carrying us. He also stopped on a dime and handled very well.

The country flattened out, and was very open. We traveled along in a slow trot and made good time.

"I think this might be the smoothest traveling horse I've ever ridden," I commented.

"Seems like," Brian agreed.

"I wonder why he was so eager to sell him?" I asked. "This horse is worth some money."

"Mebbe he didn't know what he had."

I grunted in response, and we traveled on.

Occasionally Brian's big sombrero would hit me in the back of the head, and I frowned irritably.

"Soon as it's possible, I suggest you get rid of that hat," I complained.

"I don't like it anymore than you do, but it's better than a sunburn," Brian replied.

"I reckon it is," I agreed.

"Where are we headed?" Brian changed the subject.

"I've been pondering that," I replied. "I think it's time we paid Ike a visit."

"What for?"

"I'm ready to end this once and for all," I grumbled. "I'm tired of going after the small fry. I want Ike."

"But Yancy said he wanted the entire outfit."

"We cut off the head of the snake, and the rest of the body will die," I declared. "Besides, I don't care what Yancy wants. What I want is to get Jessica's hotel back."

"And killing Ike will do that?"

"Him, and some others."

It was silent as Brian thought on that.

"All right," he finally said. "I've gone this far; might as well see it to the end."

I nodded, and we traveled on.

167

The day passed quickly, and we covered a lot of ground. By late afternoon some brush started showing up, and the ground got rougher.

There was a draw in front of us that was covered with thick mesquite trees. As we trotted up I searched the bank, looking for an open spot.

Normally, a horse will slow down naturally when he comes up to some brush, but our horse didn't. Instead, he plowed right into the brush, and the sharp thorns tore at us.

"What in the world!" Brian exclaimed.

The thick brush stumbled the horse, and he almost fell. He lunged forward to keep his footing, and the jump caused Brian to fall off. He landed in the middle of a mesquite bush and yelled as the sharp thorns tore at him.

Meanwhile, the horse regained his footing, and I pulled him up and dismounted.

"What's wrong with that horse?" Brian scowled as he gingerly picked his way out of the brush.

"I'm not sure," I said.

I moved up beside the horse's head, and he just stood there calmly as if nothing had happened.

I studied his eyes, and there was a grayish tint in them. I waved my hand in front of his eye, but he showed no reaction.

I frowned and moved my hand closer, and when I was a few inches from his eye he finally saw my movements.

"This horse is almost blind!" I announced, and added bitterly, "That Mexican tricked us."

Brian groaned and shook his head.

"It wasn't a trick," he muttered. "He said 'he no look so good', remember?"

I pinched my face in thought.

"He did say that, didn't he," I grudgingly admitted.

"He sure did."

It was silent as we thought on that. I was irritated, but Brian chuckled. I finally had to chuckle with him, and we climbed back on the horse and took off.

***

I found out real quick that traveling through brush was going to be difficult. Usually, a horse just naturally makes his way through the brush. But, with a blind horse, it was up to me to make every decision. I had to guide him every step of the way, and we had to slow to a walk.

We went a few miles, and I sighed loudly.

"What's the matter?" Brian asked from behind me.

"Plenty. We're two ex-jailbirds, wearing somebody else's clothes, riding double on a blind horse. *That* is what's the matter," I said sourly, and added, "It can't get any worse than this."

"I wish you'd quit saying that," Brian grumbled, and then he pointed out, "At least we're not in prison anymore."

"I reckon so," I reluctantly agreed. "But still. Less than a month ago, we were the owners of the fanciest hotel in Texas. Now look at us. What went wrong?"

"I'd say a lot."

"All I know is that it's Ike's fault, and he's going to pay for it," I declared.

I felt Brian's sombrero hit me in the back of my head as he nodded, and it fell silent.

We traveled a few miles, and I heard Brian chuckle softly.

"What's so funny?" I asked.

"Nothing much. This blind horse just reminds me of a story I once heard."

"Let's hear it," I said to pass the time.

"Well, there was this blind porcupine that fell in love with a cactus-."

"Never mind," I interrupted with a sigh.

169

Chapter fifty-five

We named the horse No-see-ums, and the name sort of stuck. Gentle as he was, it was hard not to like him.

We took turns riding in the saddle. It was tense work, guiding No-see-ums along, and we had to pay attention.

We traveled for several weeks. We wanted to avoid any people, so we circled any towns that we came across.

Whenever we needed food we would just stop and hunt. There was plenty of deer around, and we'd cook up enough meat to last a few days. When that ran out, we would just stop again.

We finally reached Empty-lake, but we didn't ride in. Instead, we circled the town and headed towards Ike Nash's headquarters.

I had a strong urge to ride in and see April and June. I missed them both, but I kept my feelings to myself.

We camped that night about a mile from Ike's headquarters. We were now on Ike's range, so we didn't risk the chance of a fire.

We were in no hurry, and we slept late the next morning. We sipped water from our canteens and chewed on some deer meat, and then we saddled No-see-ums and took out.

We had only ridden about a hundred yards when we spotted a rider. He was trotting briskly, coming from the direction of Ike's headquarters.

He spotted us, and he changed his course and headed in our direction.

"This can't be good," I frowned.

I felt Brian's sombrero hit me in the head as he nodded.

I placed my gun hand on my Colt handle as the rider drew close. He was looking at us curiously, and I suddenly recognized him.

"That's Ross Stewart!" I hissed in surprise.

"Sure is," Brian said.

170

Ross trotted on up to us, and we could tell that he was wary. But then he recognized us, and his eyes grew wide.

Ross was visibly shaken, and he stared at us with his mouth open. First he studied Brian, and then he looked at me.

"What happened to you two?" He finally asked.

"What do you mean?" I asked innocently.

"Where have you two been? Rondo's been worried sick."

"We've been around," I said, and my face was emotionless.

"What are you two wearing?"

"Clothes," I said matter-of-factly.

"Last I knew you two were going after Brock and Amos, but then you just disappeared!"

"We had a little run of bad luck."

"I can see that," Ross said, and asked, "Did you hear that Yancy and Cooper arrested Brock and Amos?"

"We heard that," I nodded.

"Word just came that they escaped from Huntsville."

"You don't say," I said, and Brian and I tried to look surprised.

Ross started to say something else, but I cut him off and changed the subject.

"What are you doing out here on Ike's range?"

"I was delivering a message."

"You're running errands for Ike now?" I frowned disapprovingly.

"Not usually. But, some big politician from back east is in town," Ross explained. "Feller named Ron Gallegan. He asked me to come tell Ike that he was staying at the hotel, and Rondo thought it was a good idea. He figures Brock and Amos will head this way, so this gave us an excuse to look around."

"Did you find them?"

"Nope."

171

I nodded and asked, "How's April and June?"

"They're fine," Ross replied. "April is still working at the hotel. She and Jeremiah have become friendly."

"Friendly?" I scowled.

"Sure," Ross nodded "Jeremiah has been real nice to her. June too."

"I bet he has," I grumbled, and my face turned dark.

"Are you boys riding into town?" Ross asked.

"No, we've got some business to take care of first."

"Oh? What business?" Ross looked suspicious.

"Nothing much," I replied nonchalantly. "You go on to town. We'll be along directly."

Ross didn't like it, but he still nodded.

"I'll see you boys later," he said.

We nodded, and he kicked up his horse.

We watched him leave, and then I kicked up No-see-ums. He broke into a gentle trot, and we headed towards Ike's ranch headquarters.

Chapter fifty-six

It was early in the morning when Ross Stewart rode up to Ike's headquarters. He looked around curiously as he walked his horse up to the main house, and Butch Nelson met him at the porch.

Ross delivered his message, and then he left, going back towards town.

Butch went inside and entered the study. Ike was seated at his desk, eating breakfast and studying a map.

"Morning, Ike."

"Butch," Ike nodded, and he gestured at the map spread out before him. "Come look at this."

Butch walked over to the desk and peered down.

There were little circles drawn all over the map, representing the ranches that Ike owned. Ike placed his finger on one of these circles that was to the west.

"I just bought this ranch last month," Ike reminded.

"The Johnson's place," Butch nodded.

Ike moved his finger north and tapped his finger on another circle.

"I bought this ranch last year."

"I remember," Butch said. "He didn't want to sell at first."

"Most of them don't."

Butch nodded, and Ike moved his finger back to the south and tapped again between the two circles.

"If I owned this ranch, then all three ranches would be connected."

"That would be a big spread," Butch agreed.

"Go talk to the owner, and see if he's willing to sell," Ike said as he leaned back in his chair. "Leave a few men here, but take the rest. Seeing all our men might help convince him to sell."

"I'll leave soon as the boys finish their breakfast," Butch said.

Ike nodded, satisfied. A few seconds passed, and Butch cleared his throat.

"There's news from town."

"Oh?"

"That politician friend of yours. He's at the hotel."

"Good!" Ike said, pleased. "Have somebody saddle my horse. I'll ride in and see him after breakfast."

Butch nodded and started towards the door.

Ike watched him leave, and he grunted in satisfaction. He took a swig of coffee and returned to his map.

Chapter fifty-seven

Ross was curious and concerned as he rode into Empty-lake. He dismounted at the jail, tied his horse to the railing, and hurried inside.

Rondo Landon sat at his desk, going over some papers. He looked up and was surprised to see Ross.

"Back so soon?"

"I got here quick as I could."

"You found Brock and Amos?" Rondo looked hopeful.

"No, but you're going to be surprised when I tell you who I *did* see."

"Who?"

"Lee Mattingly and Brian Clark," Ross announced, and Rondo jumped in surprise.

"Where are they?"

"They were headed towards Ike's headquarters," Ross said, and then he explained about their meeting.

Rondo frowned in thought and asked, "I wonder what happened to them?"

"I don't know, but they looked horrible. They hadn't shaved in weeks. In fact, the only thing that looked good was their horse," Ross said, and asked, "Why would they go to Ike's headquarters?"

"I don't know, but we'd better find out," Rondo said somberly as he stood. "Let's go."

Ross nodded and followed him out the door.

Chapter fifty-eight

We rode up on a hilltop that overlooked Ike's ranch headquarters. We pulled up and studied the layout.

Things were busy. There were around twenty men a-horseback, and they were leaving headquarters in a brisk trot, going west.

I squinted my eyes at them. I wasn't sure, but it looked like Butch was leading them.

We watched as they disappeared over the skyline, and then we turned our attention back to headquarters.

I spotted a saddled horse, tied to the hitching rail at the main house, and there were also at least four men down at the barn.

"You know we could get killed down there," Brian spoke up.

"It's possible," I agreed. I sighed and added, "The sad truth of it, Brian, is that it just doesn't matter much to me anymore."

"It matters to me," Brian objected. It was silent, and then he sighed. "Well, nothing lasts forever."

"We've had our ups and downs, but I've enjoyed it," I said, and I turned in the saddle and offered my hand.

Brian shook my hand firmly and nodded.

"You ready?" I asked.

"I'm as ready as I'm going to get," he said.

I smiled faintly. We checked our weapons, and then I nudged No-see-ums forward.

***

The men at the barn spotted us as we trotted down the hill. They grabbed their rifles and walked towards the main house.

Ike Nash appeared from the porch. He was headed towards the saddled horse, but he stopped abruptly when he spotted us. His four men joined him, and they spread out into a line as we rode up.

"Stop right there," Ike said gruffly.

"I'm stopped," I replied, and I pulled up No-see-ums.

Ike's eyes grew wide when he recognized us.

"What happened to you two?" He asked.

"Oh, a little of this, and a little of that," I replied.

"What are you doing here?" Ike wanted to know.

I didn't reply as we dismounted. I dropped my reins and stepped forward, and Brian stood by my side, holding his rifle with the barrel pointed down at the ground.

I heard a soft click as he pulled the hammer back, and my hand hovered over my Colt's handle.

No-see-ums didn't move. Instead, he dropped his head and snipped at the grass.

"We came here to see you," I finally said.

"What about?"

"You made a mistake, taking our hotel."

Ike frowned thoughtfully, and several seconds passed.

"You rode all the way out here just to tell me that?"

"No. We came here to get it back."

Surprise showed in Ike's face.

"I see," he said thoughtfully. "Did you bring any money with you?"

"No, you already have all our money."

"What do you mean by that?"

"I think you know," I replied.

Ike nodded slowly and asked, "What if I don't want to give the hotel back?"

"That would be another mistake."

"No," Ike smiled wolfishly. "You're the one who made the mistake."

"How's that?"

"You didn't bring any men with you."

177

I smiled at that.

"That's the difference between you and me."

"What's that?" Ike looked curious.

"I don't hire my killing done."

Ike grunted, and a pleased look crossed his face.

"Is that all you think I am?" He asked.

"Pretty much."

"I don't wear this Colt just for looks," he said. "I know how to use it."

"Thanks for the warning."

Suddenly, Ike's face turned dark.

"You were there when my son Tanner was killed."

"I sure was."

"Well then, I should be thanking you."

"For what?"

"I'm a patient man, and I've been waiting for a chance to get back at you, Ross, and Rondo. And now here you are, trespassing on my land."

"I'm glad I could help."

It was silent then, and every second seemed like an hour. I stared into Ike's eyes, and my nerves, muscles, and guts inside me were bunched up tight in anticipation.

Ike's face was pale and tight-drawn, but controlled. He stood rigid, and a harsh coldness was coming over him.

His eyes suddenly blinked, and we grabbed for our Colts.

Ike was fast. We brought our six-shooters up at the same time, and our shots blended together.

I heard a loud thump as my bullet hit flesh, and Ike flew backwards and landed on his back.

I also felt a wicked blow hit me somewhere below, and I staggered backwards but managed to stay on my feet.

Gunshots erupted around me, and in the corner of my eye I saw Brian stagger as he took lead. But he was also firing his Henry furiously, and I heard a scream of pain.

Ike was trying to raise himself up, so I fired again. My bullet caught him in the chest, and he was flipped over backwards.

I started to turn to the others, but before I could another bullet slammed into my shoulder and threw me backwards. I landed hard on my back, but I managed to keep ahold of my Colt.

Brian was down on one knee beside me. He had dropped his rifle, but now he held his Colt and was still firing away.

Two of Ike's men were still standing, and they were firing at us. While lying there I fired twice at the closest one, and his body jerked backwards. Meanwhile, Brian took care of the other one, and they fell at the same time.

I turned my attention to the other two, but they were down for good.

I heard a grimace beside me. I looked sideways and saw Brian fall over onto his back.

I was about to say something when I heard a noise. I looked and spotted a man running out of the bunkhouse. He disappeared around the corner, and a few seconds later he reappeared. He was a-horseback, and he was riding out in a dead run.

With pain everywhere, I managed to get up on one knee. Breathing hard, I lifted my Colt and aimed. I emptied my six-shooter at the fleeing man, but his horse never broke stride as he rode up the hill and disappeared.

I grimaced as I lowered the Colt. I was dizzy, so I allowed myself to fall gently onto my back. With my elbows on the ground and my hands pointed upward, I stared up at the blue sky and breathed.

"Brian?" I gasped.

"I'm here," came the abrupt answer.

"Hit bad?"

"I think so. You?"

"Not sure yet."

"They all dead?"

I glanced sideways at them.

"They ain't moving."

"Good."

"Let me catch my breath," I gasped. "Then I'll see what I can do."

"All right," Brian sounded tired. "Don't die on me."

"I'll try. You don't die either."

Brian grunted, and then it was silent.

I'm not sure when it happened, but I must have passed out after that because I don't remember anything else.

Chapter fifty-nine

I woke up to pain. My head hurt, my ribs hurt; it even hurt to breath.

I also heard a familiar snoring, and I was relieved to hear it.

My eyes were dry and matted, but I forced them open anyhow. I blinked a few times before I spotted a ceiling above me.

I was in a bunk. I turned my head and spotted Brian Clark sleeping in another bunk.

Moving slowly, I felt at my right hip, and a wave of panic came over me when I realized that I wasn't wearing my Colt.

With considerable pain, I swung my feet out and sat up. The movement caused my head to swirl, and I had to close my eyes as I gathered myself.

Several minutes passed, and I opened my eyes again and looked around.

I was in a bunkhouse. The room looked familiar, but I couldn't place where I was.

I spotted my gun-belt and Colt on another bunk, and there was also a new shirt and pants folded beside them.

There was a noise at the door. A young man walked in, and he was small, lean, and had red hair. He looked familiar, but I couldn't place him.

"You're awake!" He said loudly, and I winced as a sharp pain exploded in my head.

"Not so loud," I managed to say.

"Sorry," he said, and asked, "How do you feel?"

I grunted in response.

"Where are we?" I asked.

"You don't know?" He looked at me with an amused look.

"No."

"You're at Mr. Tomlin's ranch headquarters," he informed. "Rondo Landon brought you here."

"Rondo?"

"Sure, him and Ross. You were in bad shape. You had a bullet in your shoulder and another one stuck between two ribs. Mrs. Tomlin dug 'em out though."

"How 'bout Brian?"

"He got hit in the leg, hip, and arm. You boys were sure lucky."

I grunted at that.

"What happened to my horse?" I asked suddenly.

"Is he the blind one?"

"That's him."

"He's fine. He's down at the barn."

I nodded and asked, "Where's Rondo?"

"In town. He should be here tonight."

I was confused about a lot of things. I shook my head to clear the cobwebs, and I winced as sharp pains shot through my body.

"Who are you?" I asked as I tried to ignore the pain.

"You don't recognize me?"

"I do, I just can't think straight right now."

"I'm Rory. Rory Wheeler."

I nodded slowly as my memory came back.

"You work for Mr. Tomlin."

"That's right."

"Is Mr. Tomlin here?"

"No. He's out."

I frowned as I tried to force myself to think. But I was just too tired, and with a sigh I leaned back on my bunk.

"You don't look so good," Rory said. "Why don't you get some more rest? Rondo can explain everything later."

"I think that's a good idea."

Rory nodded and left the bunkhouse. Meanwhile, I closed my eyes and drifted off.

Chapter sixty

I woke up a few hours later.

Brian was awake too. He was sitting up, eating a bowl of soup, and he grinned when he saw me.

"Well! You're still alive," he said.

"And you still snore," I managed to smile back.

"Hungry?"

"I could eat."

"There's a pot of soup on the stove."

I nodded. I breathed deeply and tried to stand, but I was too wobbly and dizzy. With a grimace I eased back down, and Brian smiled.

"Stay there. I'll get it."

I nodded gratefully, and Brian put his bowl down and limped over to the stove. He fixed me a bowl of soup, grabbed a spoon, and hobbled back to me.

"Thanks," I said as I took the bowl.

Brian nodded and sat back down on his bunk. I suddenly realized how hungry I was, and it was silent as we ate.

"That was a violent gunfight," Brian finally said.

"I reckon it was," I agreed.

"We were lucky."

"I suppose we were," I said, and then I smiled. "Mebbe our luck is changing."

Brian grunted as we ate some more soup.

***

Rondo rode in that evening, and he looked relieved to see us awake and sitting up.

"Well! It looks like you boys are going to make it," he smiled at us. "We were worried for a few days."

"I wasn't," I smiled.

"No, you weren't worried about anything," Rondo chuckled.

"What all happened?" I asked.

"Well, Ross rode into town all worried, so we rode out to Ike's headquarters. We found Ike and four of his men dead, and you two were passed out. We borrowed a wagon and brought you here. Mrs. Tomlin patched you up while we went back and buried Ike and his men."

"What about Butch?" I asked curiously.

"Last I heard, he was back at Ike's headquarters. He's not saying much, and neither are his men."

I frowned as I thought on that.

"Well, Butch never did do me much harm," I figured. "As long as he doesn't cause me any trouble, I won't go after him."

"I'm glad to hear you say that," Rondo replied. "Besides, you're in enough trouble as it is."

"What do you mean?" I narrowed my eyes.

"One of Ike's hands got away," Rondo explained. "He came riding into town, yelling that you and Brian shot Ike down in cold blood."

"That ain't exactly how it happened," I corrected.

"I know that, but the damage has been done," Rondo continued. "There's some bigwig politician from back east in town, and he and Ike were friends. He's demanding justice. He's written letters back east, telling everybody what you did, and he's also been in to see me several times demanding that I do something."

I scowled and shook my head in disgust.

"So what happens now?" Brian spoke up.

"You boys should be safe here for a few weeks. But, soon as you're able to ride, I suggest you boys clear out until things settle down."

"What are you going to do about the politician?" I asked.

"I told him I'd look around, but I also told him that Lee Mattingly knows how to cover his tracks."

I smiled at that, and then a curious look crossed my face. "How about Ross? Does he go along with that?"

"He'll do whatever I tell him."

"What does that mean?"

"It means just that," Rondo said, and then he changed the subject. "You boys are short on equipment, so I took an extra saddle and two horses from Ike. He won't be needing them anymore. They're at the barn, and Mr. Tomlin bought you both some new clothes and two new hats."

"I appreciate that."

"That about covers everything on my end," Rondo said, and then he asked, "Now, where have you two been? What happened?"

"Do you want the short version or the long one?" I smiled faintly.

Chapter sixty-one

Recovery was a slow process, and during the next few weeks we took several long naps and played a lot of poker.

We finally started feeling better. We were still stiff and sore, but at least we could move around some.

Rondo rode out to see us one evening, and he looked worried.

"That politician is still stirring up trouble," he told us. "He's demanding that you two hang for killing Ike."

"I don't think I'd like that," I frowned.

"Can you boys ride?" Rondo asked.

"I can," Brian spoke up. "How about you, Lee?"

I nodded slowly.

"We could leave in the morning," Brian suggested.

"No," I shook my head. "There's something I've got to do first."

"What?" Rondo asked.

"We came back here to get our hotel back," I reminded, and Rondo frowned disapprovingly.

"How are you planning on doing that?" He asked.

"I once rode into town and delivered a message for you," I explained. "Remember?"

"You delivered a message to Palmer," he recollected.

"That's right," I nodded, and asked, "Care to return the favor?"

"Who's the message for?"

"Jeremiah Wisdom."

Rondo frowned thoughtfully and asked, "What's the message?"

"Tell him I'll be coming to see him in the morning."

Rondo looked hesitant.

"Are you sure about this? I've got to know him some, and he isn't all that bad a feller."

"He was in cahoots with Ike," I replied in a curt voice.

186

Rondo studied me for several seconds, and then he nodded.

"All right, I'll tell him."

"I appreciate it."

"Promise me one thing," Rondo added. "Talk to him first."

"What for?"

"You might be surprised and work something out."

I had my doubts, but I agreed for Rondo's sake.

"All right. I'll talk to him," I said.

Rondo nodded and turned to leave.

"Watch out for that politician," he warned me.

"I will," I promised, and Rondo left.

Chapter sixty-two

We saddled our horses after breakfast the next morning.

Rondo had a good eye for horseflesh. He'd picked us out two good-looking horses, and they were real gentle too.

We thanked the Tomlins for taking us in, and then we climbed on our horses and took out.

We used No-see-ums as a packhorse, and he trotted along close behind my horse.

Even though the bouncing hurt, it felt good to be back in the saddle. It also felt good to be wearing normal clothes again.

We were silent as we trotted along. Brian looked like he wanted to say something, but he never did.

We finally arrived at town. The streets were mostly empty, and nobody paid us much attention.

A cold, empty feeling grabbed at me as we walked our horses down the main street. Seeing our hotel brought back a lot of memories, and I felt a pinch in my stomach.

We dismounted in front of the hotel, and I looped my reins around the hitching rail and tied them in a slipknot. Brian did the same, and then we checked our weapons. I looked at him and nodded, and we stepped up onto the front porch.

The oak doors were open and pushed back. We walked through the swinging doors, and I stood to the side while my eyes adjusted.

I took a long, slow look around, and I frowned thoughtfully.

The floors were clean, the bar shined, and all the glassware shone. Everything was neat and tidy and organized.

A new, fancy glass mirror hung behind the bar. I studied it a moment, and then I heard a movement from the kitchen.

It was April, and June was trailing behind her.

April spotted us, and a warm look crossed her face. June was happy too, and her eyes shone brightly.

My heart jumped. In a mere matter of seconds, I was flooded with all sorts of confusing emotions.

I started to smile, but then I remembered why I was here.

April noticed my somber look, and her grin vanished.

I looked past them and spotted Jeremiah Wisdom. He was sitting at my corner table, and he had a game of solitaire laid out in front of him.

I took in a big breath and walked towards him while Brian stayed at the door.

I glanced at April, and she looked worried.

I turned my eyes back to Jeremiah. He just sat there calmly, looking up at me with his hands on the table.

"Stand up," I said quietly, and my voice carried well in the empty room.

"I don't want to fight you, Lee," he said calmly.

"You'll have to," I replied roughly. "I came here to get my hotel back."

"Why?" Jeremiah asked abruptly.

I was taken back by the question, and several seconds passed as I thought on that.

"Because it's mine," I finally said.

"No, it's not," Jeremiah said matter-of-factly, and then he added, "Even if you got it back, you can't stay here. You're a wanted man."

"I'll worry about that later," I said, and I lowered my gun hand over my gun handle.

Jeremiah saw my movements, but he didn't move.

"You're a reasonable man, Lee," he said. "What happened with Ike; that's debatable. But this isn't right, and you know it."

"You were in cahoots with Ike," I accused.

"I was," Jeremiah admitted. "But, everything I did was legal."

"You cheated me at cards."

"No, I didn't."

"You expect me to believe that?" I raised an eyebrow.

"I don't have to cheat."

I frowned thoughtfully, and then I changed the subject.

"It's doesn't matter," I said. "I lost something that didn't belong to me, and that's why I'm here."

Jeremiah looked intrigued.

"What are you talking about?"

"The hotel was only partly ours," I explained. "We had a silent partner, and it wasn't her fault we lost the hotel."

"Her?"

I frowned irritably, and with a sigh I replied, "Jessica Tussle. She was our partner."

Jeremiah nodded slowly.

"She's the lady who showed up the day you lost the hotel."

"That's right."

It fell silent as Jeremiah thought on that.

"I'm a reasonable man," he finally said. "So, before there's any trouble, I have a proposal."

"Let's hear it."

"If I understand this correctly, you're only here because of Jessica."

"That would be correct, yes."

"All right then. I'll give Jessica her part of the hotel back, and I'll be her new partner. I'll offer her the same deal that you and Brian had."

I glanced over at Brian, and he nodded slightly. I looked at April next, and the expression on her face was begging me to accept the offer.

"All right," I said softly. "The hotel's yours and Jessica's."

Jeremiah smiled pleasantly, but I didn't return the smile. Instead, I turned and looked at April, and our eyes locked.

Several long seconds passed, but April and I didn't seem to notice.

I was about to say something when a man wearing a fancy vest burst through the door. The swinging door caught Brian in the back, and the impact knocked him over.

He held a rifle, and he also had a wild look in his eyes.

He spotted me standing there, and with an outraged yell he swung his rifle up.

Chapter sixty-three

He fired before I could do anything, and I heard a sharp whip as a bullet flew by my head and hit the wall behind me.

I jumped sideways, drew my Colt, aimed instinctively, and pulled the trigger. The Colt bucked in my hand, and I heard a loud thump as my bullet hit flesh.

The man in the fancy vest was slammed backwards, and he hit the bar and slid to the ground. He kicked out, made a few gurgling sounds, and then was still.

There was a stunned silence in the room. Smoke from my Colt lifted, and I took the spent shell out and reloaded it with a fresh one.

We heard running footsteps, and Rondo and Ross burst through the swinging doors with their Colts in hand.

Rondo looked around the room, and then he glanced down at the dead man. His face turned dark as he studied him.

"Did you kill him?" He looked at me.

"I had no choice," I replied.

Rondo made a groaning sound and shook his head.

"This isn't good," he said. "This is Ron Gallegan, the politician I was telling you about."

"But it was self defense!" April spoke up, and everybody nodded.

"It's not going to matter," Rondo muttered and looked at me. "You'd better leave, Lee, and don't come back for a long time."

I nodded and holstered my Colt. I glanced at Jeremiah, and he smiled apologetically.

"I'll tell Jessica she has a new partner," I told him. "She'll be in touch."

"I'm looking forward to working with her," Jeremiah replied.

I nodded and turned towards April. June was hiding behind her, and she peered at me from behind April's skirt.

My legs felt heavy as I walked over to them. April took a small step forward, and it was silent as we stared at each other.

At that moment, I didn't care about anything else. To me April was the most beautiful woman I'd ever seen, and my heart ached.

Her face was soft and hopeful and terribly vulnerable. She smiled, and her eyes were honest and direct.

"You have to go," she said softly.

"I'm afraid so," I said reluctantly.

"Will you come back someday?" She asked hopefully.

"I just might."

"Good," April flashed me a smile. "We'll be here."

I suddenly felt a huge lump in my throat. I nodded, and with a heavy voice I said, "Goodbye, April."

"Take care of yourself," she said.

"I will," I said, and then I looked down at June. "Take care of your Ma, June."

She didn't reply. Instead, she just stared at me through those big, blue eyes.

I smiled at her, and then I turned and walked towards the door.

Brian followed me outside, and we untied our horses and climbed into the saddle. Meanwhile, everyone else came out onto the porch and watched us.

I looked at Rondo, and he nodded at me.

"I'll be seeing you," he said.

"Sooner or later," I agreed, then I looked at April.

She smiled bravely, and I smiled back. A few seconds passed, and then I tipped my hat at her and nudged my horse forward.

I tugged on my lead rope. No-see-ums fell in behind me obediently, and Brian brought up the rear.

As our horses went down the street I heard June say softly, "Mister Lee, please don't go. *Please.*"

My heart ached as I kicked my horse up to a trot.

Epilogue

We traveled north for two days. Our camps were dry, and we ate canned goods.

No-see-ums worked great as a packhorse. He followed close behind my horse and caused us no problems.

We finally figured that we had ridden far enough. Our third night out we made camp, built a fire, and cooked supper. We tore into the hot meal with a vengeance, and afterwards we sat round the fire and drank coffee.

"You ain't mentioned it, but where are we headed?" Brian broke the silence.

"Midway."

"Oh?" Brian looked intrigued. "What for?"

"We need to talk to Jessica."

"Talk to her about what?"

"Tell her the hotel is hers again," I explained.

"Oh. That," Brian nodded, and asked, "Is there anything else you plan on saying to her?"

"I have nothing else *to* say," I frowned and added, "Besides, she's made her choice. She made that clear. And, I wouldn't choose her now anyway."

Brian nodded and asked, "I wonder if Yancy knows that?"

"I don't care if he does or not," I retorted. "It makes no difference to me."

Brian studied me thoughtfully and cleared his throat.

"I'm going to miss April and that kid," he said as he changed the subject.

I felt a tension in my chest. The mere mention of April's name made me feel miserable.

I didn't say anything as I took a swig of coffee.

"Judging from the looks on their faces when we lit out, I'd say they'll miss us too," Brian mused out loud.

"Perhaps."

195

"If you'd have asked her, I think she would have come with us," Brian declared.

"No," I disagreed. "She wouldn't have done that."

"How can you be so sure?" He raised an eyebrow.

"We're two outlaws on the run," I pointed out. "What sort of life would that be? She also has June to look after."

"Coming with us would have been better than being alone," Brian objected.

"She's not alone," I said bitterly. "She and Jeremiah seemed to be getting along just fine."

"I'm not so sure about that."

"It doesn't matter," I replied, and my voice was husky. "They're better off without us."

Brian frowned thoughtfully, and it fell silent as we drank our coffee.

"So, after Midway, then what?" Brian asked after a while.

"I've no plans," I shrugged. "I reckon we'll just see what develops."

"Are you planning on returning to the outlaw way of life?" Brian looked curiously at me.

"We *are* outlaws, whether we like it or not," I shrugged.

"I reckon you're right," he said wistfully, and added, "All I know is that I don't ever want to go back to prison."

"Me either," I agreed.

"If I had known what prison life was like when I was younger, I would have changed my ways."

I smiled faintly, and it was silent for a while.

"Well, think I'll turn in," Brian finally said, and I nodded in agreement.

We rolled out our bedrolls, pulled our boots off, and crawled in. Brian started snoring a few minutes later, but I tossed and turned.

My thoughts drifted to April and June.

As if they were standing in front of me, I kept picturing them as we rode out of town. April stared at me through those big, blue eyes, and June kept saying, 'Mister Lee, please don't go. *Please*'.

I sighed. That June had the most innocent face and softest voice I had ever heard.

It was an image that would haunt me for a long time.

Author's note

It was too tempting not to include a cameo appearance by John Wesley Hardin.

Hardin is considered to be one of the most deadly gunfighters Texas has ever known, and it's rumored that he once killed a man just for snoring.

His numerous attempts to escape from Huntsville have been well documented. He came close several times but never succeeded, and he eventually adapted to prison life.

While serving his sentence he studied Law, and he passed the state's bar examination and obtained his license when he was released in 1894.

In August 1895, John Selman, Sr, in El Paso, Texas, shot and killed Hardin. In 2002, the bullet that killed Hardin was sold at a private auction for $80,000.

Lee and Brian's escape from Huntsville is also based loosely on true events. However, the actual attempt failed when the escapees were found and arrested a few days later while attempting to steal a horse from a nearby Mexican village.

About the Author

Born in West Texas, Tell Cotten is a seventh generation Texan. He comes from a family with a ranching heritage and is a member of the Sons of the Republic of Texas. Besides writing, he is also in the cattle business, and he resides in West Texas with his wife, Andi, and their two children.

Tell has enjoyed writing from an early age, and he also has a great love of the history of the west. LEE is his sixth novel in The Landon Saga series.

For announcements of new releases and all other information, please join The Landon Saga Facebook group https://www.facebook.com/groups/784798154926122/ or join Tell Cotten's website http://tellcotten.wordpress.com/

Acknowledgements
I would like to thank my wife and family for all their help and support. Without them this wouldn't be possible.

I'd also like to thank Bill for the fantastic drawing, and thanks to Mike for putting the cover together.

A special thanks also goes out to Jerry for his resourceful knowledge.

And lastly, I'd like to thank Melissa for all her advice, help, and hard work.

Enjoy this excerpt from Tell Cotten's upcoming novel:

They Rode Together
Book seven in The Landon Saga series

It was a surprise town council meeting, hastily thrown together.

Rondo Landon rarely liked surprises, and he was skeptical when Ross came and told him.

"What's this all about?" He asked as they walked down the street.

"All Fred Stilwell told me is to fetch you," Ross replied. "He said they had something important to discuss."

Rondo frowned, but didn't reply.

Rondo Landon was the sheriff of Empty-lake, and Ross was his deputy. Rondo was small and hard bodied, and he was also well known for the ivory-handled Colt that he always displayed on his right hip.

As for Ross, he had a tall and lanky frame, with tanned skin and brown hair. When he spoke he always displayed a rich, Texan drawl.

The meeting was being held at the jail. This irritated Rondo, because the jail was *his* office, not the town council's.

They passed Rondo's house, and his wife Rachel was sitting out on the front porch.

She had long, brown hair with sandy looking freckles that covered her face. She also had a knowing smile that always made Rondo squirm, and she was giving him that look now.

Despite his foul mood, Rondo couldn't help but smile back.

"Where are you two headed?" She asked.

Rondo gestured at the jail.

"Town council wants to hold a meeting."

"Can I come?"

"Why not," Rondo said.

Rachel smiled and bounded off the porch. She walked beside Rondo, and they held hands as they went to the jail.

The town council had three members, and they were all waiting. There was also another man there, and Rondo frowned irritably when he spotted him.

He was sitting in Rondo's chair, and he had his feet up on his desk.

He had a leathery face with a hard jaw and cold eyes. He was a tall man, and despite the smirk on his face, there was no kindness in him. He wore a Colt on his hip, and he looked comfortable wearing it.

The mood was somber, and Rondo was suspicious. They'd had meetings before, but not like this.

"What is this?" He demanded to know.

Fred Stilwell stepped forward. He looked nervous as he cleared his throat.

"Rondo, we consider you to be a good friend. The first thing we want to say is that we really appreciate the job you've done. The way you handled Ike's men was impressive. *Very* impressive."

"Thanks," Rondo said stiffly.

"But," Fred added, "We're extremely disappointed with how you handled the situation with Lee Mattingly."

"What situation?"

The man behind the desk swung his feet off the desk, stood, and walked over.

"Allow me to explain," he said in a hard, curt voice. "You did nothing as Lee Mattingly rode into town and murdered Ron Gallegan. And, to make matters worse, afterwards you encouraged Lee to leave. You should have arrested him and Brian Clark both."

"And who are you?" Rondo narrowed his eyes.

"Folks call me Rock. Rock Bullen."

Rondo had heard of him, but he hid his surprise.

201

Rock was a known bounty hunter, and his methods were harsh.

"It was self defense," Rondo argued.

"No, it was murder," Rock replied, and added, "Besides, that's not for you to decide. Your job is to arrest them. It's the Judge's job to decide who's guilty and who's not."

"If I want your opinion, I'll ask," Rondo replied curtly. "I know how to do my job."

"It's not your job anymore," Rock said, and he turned to Fred. "Ain't that right?"

Rondo turned his glare to Fred, and he looked fidgety.

"I'm sorry, Rondo," he said. "But we've got to let you go. Ron Gallegan was a very important man back east, and word is out that you and Lee are friends. It just doesn't look good, especially since you let him escape."

A heavy silence filled the room. Rondo pinched his face in thought as he looked at Rock.

"What are you doing here?" He asked.

"I've been hired to bring Lee Mattingly in, dead or alive," Rock announced smugly. "Brian Clark too."

"Good luck with that."

Rock made a grunting sound. Rondo wasn't sure, but he thought it might have been an attempt at a laugh.

Nobody had anything else to say, and the silence was uncomfortable.

Rondo was mad, but he managed to control his emotions. He nodded to himself, and he removed his sheriff's badge that was pinned on his vest.

He started to toss it onto the floor, but decided against it. Instead, he walked over to the desk and put it down gently.

Rondo turned and looked at each member of the town council. His gaze was honest and direct, and each member dropped their eyes.

He then looked at Ross, and Ross just stood there looking thoughtful and surprised.

Rondo turned to Rachel and held out his hand.

202

"Let's go," he said softly.

Rachel forced a smile. She took her husband's hand, and they walked out.

As the door shut behind them, Rondo heard Fred Stilwell say, "Ross, we'd like to talk to you."

Coming soon from Solstice Publishing

For announcements of new releases and all other information, please join The Landon Saga Facebook group https://www.facebook.com/groups/784798154926122/ or join Tell Cotten's website http://tellcotten.wordpress.com/